The Wedding Planners

Planning perfect weddings...
finding happy endings!

It's the biggest and most important day
of a woman's life—and it has to be perfect.

At least, that's what The Wedding Belles
believe, and that's why they're
Boston's top wedding planner agency.
But amidst the beautiful bouquets,
divine...
these...

h...
But fi...

This month: Melissa James
THE BRIDEGROOM'S SECRET
Planner: Julie's always been the wedding
planner—will she ever be the bride...?

And don't miss the exciting wedding
planner tips and author reminiscences
that accompany each book!

...her own unique wedding and honeymoon ... us:

'As ... as weddings go, mine was very simple. We were pretty poor, and it seemed a waste of money to me to buy an expensive dress. So I bought an ex-rental at a store for $50. We had the reception at my grandfather's bowling club. The whole wedding cost less than $2000. We started our married life in a small apartment near a prison, and our first house, a year later, was a tiny one in a run-down area. None of this made the marriage any the worse, since we've now been married almost 25 years, with three children and still going strong.

'It also seems I followed in the best tradition of **The Wedding Planners** authors and had an unusual start to my wedding, when a sudden storm broke out as we pulled up. It was blinding rain, and the chauffeur carried me into the church!

'We also didn't have the usual honeymoon destination. In a country where almost everyone chooses Bali, Fiji, The Gold Coast or the Whitsunday Islands on the Great Barrier Reef, we took a driving tour along the Bushranger Roads of our state. We hid behind Captain Thunderbolt's ("the gentleman bushranger") Rocks, stood where his woman, Maryanne, was caught, visited his folk museum and the prison he was housed in, and where his gang holed up. We also stayed in a tiny cabin in the middle of nowhere in a National Park. Romance in rustic surrounds!

'In THE BRIDEGROOM'S SECRET, you'll discover Julie's hidden talent for finding unusual honeymoon destinations. This talent changes her life…thanks to Matt. Most of the places mentioned are places I've been blessed enough to visit in my life. Since we moved to Europe, I've definitely found many new and unusual places…and amazing people wherever we go. I hope you find a few of those places and people enriching the story.'

Catch up with Melissa and her latest news at www.melissajames.net

Visit http://harlequin-theweddingplanners.blogspot.com to find out more…

THE BRIDEGROOM'S SECRET

BY
MELISSA JAMES

MILLS & BOON®

Pure reading pleasure™

For Maryanne, who had a heart as true and loving as any I've ever known.
And for the real Jules, who will grow up to be just as special as her mom.
Massive thanks to 'the girls', Shirley, Myrna, Melissa, Linda and Susan, for the creation of this series, and allowing me to take part. Thanks to Kim and Lydia for revisions that made the book better. And my deepest gratitude goes to Rachel and Robbie, who stayed up late to read for me when they both had their own deadlines. Thanks, girls. I have had and still continue to be blessed with beautiful, giving critique partners.

First published in Great Britain 2008
Harlequin Mills & Boon Limited,
Eton House, 18-24 Paradise Road, Richmond, Surrey TW9 1SR

© Lisa Chaplin 2008

ISBN: 978 0 263 86540 0

Set in Times Roman 13 on 14¼ pt
02-0908-49115

Printed and bound in Spain
by Litografia Rosés, S.A., Barcelona

The Wedding Planners

Planning perfect weddings...finding happy endings!

In April: Shirley Jump,
SWEETHEART LOST AND FOUND
Florist: will Callie catch a bouquet,
and reunite with her childhood sweetheart?

In May: Myrna Mackenzie,
THE HEIR'S CONVENIENT WIFE
Photographer: Regina's wedding album is perfect,
now she needs her husband to say I love you!

In June: Melissa McClone,
SOS MARRY ME!
Designer: Serena's already made her dress,
but a rebel has won her heart...

In July: Linda Goodnight,
WINNING THE SINGLE MUM'S HEART
Chef: who will Natalie cut her own wedding cake with...?

In August: Susan Meier,
MILLIONAIRE DAD, NANNY NEEDED!
Accountant: will Audra's budget for the big day
include a millionaire groom?

In September: Melissa James,
THE BRIDEGROOM'S SECRET
Planner: Julie's always been the wedding planner—
will she ever be the bride...?

Julie is an aspiring honeymoon planner at The Wedding Belles—here are her ideas on ways to plan a truly memorable holiday with your husband-to-be!

❦ A memorable honeymoon need not be expensive. So many people build their expectations so high that when the 'perfect' honeymoon doesn't eventuate, tears and fights do (especially over expenses)! So think about planning for what you both like to do, instead of a traditional five-star resort on an island or on the beach. A honeymoon is only a week or two—your life together lasts much longer. So choosing the destination for *you* is more important than merely 'perfect'. Your life together has already begun—if you can't afford perfect, be happy with the reality you can afford.

❦ Go for happy comfort over cranky glamour. Wear shoes that fit, sunscreen and hats, and protect yourself against wildlife/bugs.

❦ Remember, like the wedding day, the honeymoon's soon over, but the memories remain for a lifetime…good or bad. The famous saying 'there is greater happiness in giving' applies especially to your partner in life. You want to look back on your wedding/honeymoon and smile with love. And remember to laugh!

CHAPTER ONE

SO THIS was how it felt to be a queen….

Her engagement party was being held in Celebre, Boston's best restaurant—the place where Matt had first proposed to her. The champagne was flowing. There were red roses by the dozen on every table, and fairy lights lit the satin-draped walls. She wore a watered-silk dress of softest silver green and the McLachlan family diamond necklace, earrings and bracelet set, all supplied by her adoring fiancé.

Given the stress of the past nine months, after Matt's father's death and the near collapse of both his business and hers, it felt amazing that they were here now.

Well, amazing that *she* was here, anyway. Matt fitted into this world perfectly.

The cream of Boston society—all childhood friends of Matt's—filled the room and spilled out onto the terrace. Her own family hadn't been able to make it from Sydney at such short notice. But her friends, affectionately known as The Wedding Belles, because they ran a complete-wedding-package business in Boston, were here either with their own wonderful men or working the room. They were creating new business just by being there, because they were responsible for this "wedding of the year."

Her wedding.

Julie shook her head, as if to clear it. *She*, plain, publicity-shy Julie Montgomery from Rockdale, a suburb of Sydney, Australia, was the bride in what the media had dubbed Boston's Wedding of the Year. She, just a simple general assistant for The Wedding Belles, had captured the heart of Boston's most eligible bachelor. Why they'd chosen her wedding, she didn't know, any more than she knew why a man like Matt had ever fallen for someone like her.

Why she'd fallen for him was no mystery. She looked across the room at him, and her heart almost burst with pride and love. Tall and lithe, he wore the tux as though he'd been born in it, which, given his family background, he probably had been. His dark hair curled just enough to look sexily mussed; she loved the light streaks of early grey about his ears and temples, which always made her fingers ache to plunge right in there. His eyes—what woman could look into that ice-blue perfection and not do what she'd done the first minute she'd seen him? Intelligent, kind and strong, he could never see someone in need without doing something about it, whether helping out at charity events or donating funds to needy causes. If she'd fallen in love with him at a glance, she'd fallen even deeper for the man beneath, the man of integrity and generosity. He worked hard, had true creative genius, and a heart that never stopped giving.

And those *hands*…what he could do to her with a touch!

He'd been so busy lately, and, oh, how she'd missed him. But tonight was theirs, their engagement party, and he was hers alone. Needing to be near him, she smiled and detached herself from her future mother-in-law and began to go to him.

"Miss Montgomery, could we have a minute for a few questions?"

Julie held in the sigh. This was one part of her engagement she found less than appealing. As the love interest of Matthew McLachlan, president of McLachlan Marine Industries since his father's death, she was subject to public scrutiny. It was almost like being part of a second marriage. She could always count on the presence of the press in her life, during both the good times and definitely through the bad.

The Belles had come up with the idea of throwing them a wedding when it looked like Matt was going to lose the company after his father's wildly unsuccessful speculations. Since then her private love story had become public entertainment. The invitation list for the quiet family wedding The Belles had planned was now up to over 150, and the simple garden venue was now the cathedral on the harbour front, which had room for media photo shoots and the live television feed. Their wedding had become an official "human interest story," and was being followed by a top magazine, three tabloids and two TV stations covering the tristate area.

But all the media interest had also saved The Belles from going under when the high-society Vandiver wedding cancellation had left them deep in the red; so Julie's every smile for the cameras held as much gratitude and relief as it did resentment.

She turned now, with the smile that had felt more like a grimace for the past few months. "Of course… Jemima, isn't it?"

Jemima Whittaker of *Boston People Today*, the magazine covering her wedding, beamed at her. "So good of you to remember."

Remember? It was impossible not to when the woman had been in her face almost constantly for the past few months.

"So how do you feel about your fiancé's phenomenal success in saving McLachlan Marine Industries from financial flatlining?"

Her gaze flicked to Matt, talking to some people she didn't recognise in the centre of the room—probably more members of the press—and she felt her smile soften with the love she couldn't hide. "I'm incredibly proud of him, of course, but I knew he could do it. He's so dedicated to his workers and their families."

"Your fiancé didn't just save jobs, Miss Montgomery. The new water converter he's invented will revolutionise the industry." The reporter sounded one point less than smug with the information. "The new contracts with Jet Stream Industries and Red Line Marine—not to mention the giants in the motor industry showing marked interest in a land prototype—will give McLachlan's more power and wealth than it's known in its eighty-year history. Matt's done more than rescue the company from the investment mistakes of his father—

he's become a multimillionaire, is being hailed as a *wunderkind,* and has been nominated for businessman of the year after he gave shares in the converter to every McLachlan's worker that waited for their overdue salaries. Many of them are now well on their way to being rich. How do you feel about that?"

It took all of Julie's willpower to not blink or frown. Matt had enjoyed so much success in the public arena, had done so much more than save the company, and he hadn't told her? "As I said, I always knew he was a genius," she replied with another halfway-to-grimace smile, wondering why this reporter knew so much about the importance of Matt's invention, while she, his fiancée, knew nothing.

"I suppose you think so because he chose you instead of Sara Enderby or Elise Pettifer," Jemima laughed, totally without spite—probably because, like Julie herself, she came from less exalted origins than most in the room. Jemima's hand swept to where Matt stood in a crowd of people, laughing—and it was only then Julie realised that six of the eight people surrounding him were very attractive women. "You're one secure woman, obviously. If Matthew McLachlan were my fiancé, and he had two very beautiful exes making him laugh the way those women are right now, I'd drape myself over him faster than Speedy Gonzalez." She laughed again as she said, "Or kick them out of the way like that baby kangaroo on the cartoons."

The two exquisite blondes on either side of him were his *ex-girlfriends?*

Self-control. Julie held her hands at her sides, refusing to check the current state of her French twist. Her bright-red French twist. She didn't smooth her hands over her lightly applied makeup. She knew the freckles showed anyway.

"With Elise in particular, everyone was taking bets on the wedding date," Jemima went on, still without malice but with a good deal of curiosity. Digging. "She's an engineer, too, you know. In fact, I've heard rumours that she worked with him on the design of the water converter. They seemed the perfect match. That's why there was such interest when he broke up with her, and was seen with you so soon after."

A perfect match…oh, weren't they just? The handsome, high-born genius and the beautiful, high-society woman, one of his own people, who made him laugh so easily. Perfection, side by side….

Julie had met both women earlier, but hadn't

thought much about either of them afterward. They'd seemed nice women, without any sign of cattiness in their conversation or demeanour. Not by word or act had they shown anything but kindness to her.

But then, why would they need to compete, when they were so beautiful?

Then she remembered the look in Matt's eyes when he'd seen her tonight, and the world seemed to spin the right way again. "You'll have to ask Matt about who he works with and why. That's his place. Thanks for the advice, but after all, those women are in his past—I'm his future. I'm the one wearing his ring." With a cool smile she ended the interview.

But she didn't continue toward Matt. That might make it seem as if she didn't trust him, which could create fodder for a speculative story about the status of their relationship. She'd had enough of that in the past few months.

Finally the night was over, his gift to Julie. Now, after all his months of work to save McLachlan's, he could be alone with the woman he loved.

Matthew McLachlan smiled, almost bursting with the pride and love he felt. In a love story filled with obstacles—from his father's oppo-sition to Matt falling for an unknown Australian woman, to the intense media speculation, to the problems with his business and hers—Julie had risen to every occasion. She'd won everyone over with her quirky humour, her strength, grace and dignity. An extraordinary woman…and she was all his. His woman, his love.

He'd known she felt intimidated by the over-whelming media and social interest in their lives, especially since The Belles' plans for their wedding had become public knowledge. He'd seen her trepidation about tonight. Then he'd given her the dress he'd bought for her on his last trip to New York and the McLachlan diamonds his mother had brought down for her, the possession of all the future McLachlan brides. He'd seen the utter delight in being so spoiled fill her face, the excitement at being the belle of the ball, as he'd jokingly called her, playing on her job at The Wedding Belles.

Though he'd also known she didn't like all the hype, and felt she didn't quite know what to say to his high-powered friends, he could barely hold in the pride when she was nothing but herself, without an ounce of pretentiousness or trying to fit in. She'd neither clung to him, nor hidden out with her own friends, but had spent the night circulating. His mom, who'd adored Jules from the start, hadn't even had to show her future daughter-in-law the ropes of a society function. Julie had dealt with the press, the cattier members of high society, and won the approval of the older women, so hard to impress. "A lovely girl," had been the consensus he'd overheard after Jules had moved on.

She'd even chatted pleasantly with two of his ex-girlfriends, Elise and Sara, asking them about themselves, as she always did. She had such an interest in people of all walks of life. And when the press had seen the women together and had taken a picture, Matt had seen the frustration on the face of the reporter, because all three women were laughing, their body language relaxed and friendly.

"What a sensational woman," his old friend Victor had said as he left the party. "Why didn't she fall at *my* feet?" he'd muttered, with true envy in his voice.

"You're a lucky man," his other oldest friend, Guy, had added, with a quick, wistful glance at Julie.

Secure in Julie's love, Matt only grinned. Lucky...didn't he know it.

Now at last they were home, Mom had gone

tactfully to bed and, remembering the utter love in Julie's eyes as she looked at him all night, he couldn't wait anymore. "Come here, woman." He dragged her into his arms. "Do you have any idea how incredible you looked tonight? I've been dying to take this off you for hours." He lowered a strap of her dress and softly kissed her shoulder.

"Matt," she whispered as her shoulder lifted and her head fell back in the abandoned sensuality he could arouse in her with a touch.

He felt her quiver, and smiled. Hell, yes, he was a lucky man. Every day it just got better. He'd never been so happy in his life. To have a magnificent woman like Julie crazy in love with him from first sight, before she'd known who he was or what his bank balance was, had been unbelievable to him from the start.

To have her love him still, through the turbulent months where he'd sold off almost everything to prevent his mother from losing her apartment, to keep McLachlan's afloat and his workers in their jobs; to have her love him through the endless weeks when he'd been so deep in thought with the practical applications of the water converter, he'd practically forgotten she was there; to love him through a backyard engagement party and few presents, to cheerfully agree with the plans for a private wedding at City Hall to save costs—

Julie Montgomery was a walking, loving miracle, and he intended to hold on to her for life.

That's what tonight had been about. Now that he'd returned to his place in the world, McLachlan's was safe and all its workers secure, he wanted to thank her for everything, to show her off to the world for the extraordinary woman she was, to pronounce to the world that this was no temporary thing. Matt McLachlan was a one-woman man, and he was definitely taken.

Jules turned her face to his, kissing him softly, once, twice. But when he dropped the spaghetti-thin strap from her shoulder, she shook her head. "Your mother's here," she whispered.

He moved to kiss her throat in a way he knew she couldn't resist. "She knows we're lovers, Jules."

She shivered again with the touch, and Matt grinned as he bent to kiss lower.

"But it doesn't feel right," she said softly, punctuated with kisses. "I'm sorry, darling, but I can't—not with your mother in the house."

With a sigh he kissed her shoulder, and put the dress back in its place. "Ah well, she's only here for two nights. I can wait that long. You do realise I won't sleep, don't you? You're a cruel woman, Montgomery."

"Did your mother know about the importance of the water converter from the start?" she asked out of nowhere. "Or was it only when you sold it?"

Though her voice held the usual love and faith, there was a note in it—some deeper insecurity he'd never heard before—and Matt started. "What was that?"

"Your mother," she said, still smiling but with a clear worry beneath—and he wondered who'd been talking to her. "Does she know about what the water converter is, and the contracts that did far more than pull McLachlan's out of the red?"

Now totally diverted from his one-track course to the bedroom, he frowned. "I don't understand."

"It's nothing important, really. Just me being insecure." She kissed him again and smiled, her eyes full of love. Almost. The diffidence was new to her, new to him, and it niggled at him. Something was wrong. "Did you tell your mother about the water converter, and what it could mean for you, for her, for McLachlan's and all your workers, before it sold?"

Thoroughly confused now, he answered, "Well, of course. She's my mother." And it affected her financial future. She'd needed to know what was happening when the banks had started making threats to sell her apartment and the house to pay for the huge investment he'd made in the water converter.

Julie paled. "I see. Does she know how well it's doing—the multimillion-dollar contracts with the marine companies, and the possibility of the giants of the motor industry wanting a land prototype?"

"Who told you that?" he asked, startled. Who'd stolen his surprise? He'd planned tonight to the last detail. He'd been itching to tell her all about his hard work and success for weeks, and tonight had seemed the perfect time.

Now someone had stolen his rights from him, and he was furious—not with Julie, but with whoever had ruined their perfect night. When he found out who…

"Jemima Whittaker from *Boston People Today*." Julie turned her face, fiddling with the diamonds around her neck. "How long have you left me out of the loop about your invention and the contracts, Matt? I had to be told about this important part of your life by a magazine reporter who thought I knew. It was so hard to hide how surprised I was." He saw her hands come together, fingers twisting hard around each other. "It was so embarrassing. Why, Matt? Why did you tell your mother, let the media know all about it, and not me?"

He felt the colour drain from his face as he saw the sign flashing in front of him: Danger Ahead, Flash Floods. "It's been a hard time for you and The Belles during the past six months. You've been working overtime, and going through so much, trying to save your own business from disaster. I didn't want to burden you, Jules." He heard the unconvincing tone of his voice and cursed it, knowing he sounded as nervous as he felt. If that reporter had gone further, and told her the other things he'd been waiting to tell her...

"But you told your mother," she said softly, with a sadness in her voice that smote at him, making him realise he'd never thought about how she'd take his news—as surprise or secret. A secret others knew.

"I was going to tell you tonight, sweetheart." *Tell you everything, including about Kirsten and Molly, while you were in my arms, after the best night of your life. Knowing without a single doubt how much I love you.*

His best-laid plans were going awry. In that superb dress, decked out with diamonds, she'd never been lovelier—but with her drooping head and her hand jerking as she plucked at the McLachlan necklace, she looked like a wilted flower.

"We discussed this before, Matt. I want to share the bad as well as the good. I've told you about The Belles' problems, and not only when I've needed to work overtime, but what I'd be doing, why—and with whom."

The sadness in her tone told Matt he wasn't just in deep water, but in a stormy sea without a life preserver...and he realised how much he'd hurt her by his silence, not just now but for the past few months. By waiting for the right moment, instead of telling her the things she deserved to know, he'd hurt the woman he loved more than life or breath.

While he tried to prevent the shock from slowing his system, her next question broadsided him. "Jemima said there are rumours that Elise Pettifer helped you with the water converter. Are they true?"

Like a final premonition of disaster, the name echoed around and around in his head. *"Elise?"* Damn, oh, damn...

"Yes, she told me that you dated her, too, if

that's what's making you look so worried." Julie bit her lip. "Jemima said you dated her for almost a year. She's really nice, Matt. Well-bred, beautiful, and she's a fellow engineer to boot. Everyone was so shocked when you apparently ditched her for someone like me. They were waiting for the wedding date to be announced." Her eyes darkened with an emotion he didn't dare name. "So how long has she been working with you on the water converter?"

Matt broke out in a cold sweat. Dear God, she knew about his past with Elise, that he'd been working with her on a secret project, and he hadn't been the one to tell her about it. "My relationship with Elise was nothing like me and you," he said tightly. "We—damn it, it was a convenient thing. Neither of us had anyone and our parents kept throwing us together. We drifted into dating, but there was nothing there, Jules. We both agreed that if we met someone else, we'd part friends. And that's what happened."

"And she hasn't met anyone since you broke up with her—a beautiful, intelligent and lovely woman like Elise?" From gentle and trusting, Julie's voice had become brittle, and he knew he was in deep trouble.

Matt sighed. Given the way she adored him, Julie would never believe Elise didn't love him the way she did—and worse still, given her past with cheating men, she'd have a hard time believing that he'd fallen for her while dating Elise; but he couldn't let that affect him. It was time to tell her the truth.

"Elise is an old friend, and an excellent engineer. When I couldn't get my head around a major part of the job, I did ask her opinion, and she came up with a way to make it work. From there, it just—well, it all fell into place, really. We work well together but that's all."

"I understand," was all she said at first—but the pain in her voice gave him no relief, only a sinking feeling. "Were you really dating her when I kissed you that first day?" she asked, so softly he had to strain to hear her.

The spear of guilt hit him again. He wheeled away, trying to justify what was, to him, unjustifiable. "I went straight to her and told her I'd met you. We parted amicably, Jules. It was never serious between us." Could he explain that he'd never even taken Elise to bed because it felt almost like she was a sister, a cousin? He'd known her since before kindergarten; their mothers were like sisters. It just hadn't been there for him the way it was with Jules.

"Is she part of the contracts that will put McLachlan's on a worldwide map? Has she worked with you on the motoring deal?"

Palpitations, cold sweat, clenching stomach—he hadn't known extreme fear mimicked the symptoms of a heart attack until now. "Sweetheart…" He turned back to face her, knowing he might as well tell her the rest, and trust in her love to get them through. "She's an old and trusted friend, and she put thousands of dollars into the prototype that I didn't have at the time. You know how far McLachlan's had crashed. I could barely afford to pay my workers for three months. She deserved the partnership, so I got a contract made up. She owns forty percent."

"And your workers own how much?" she whispered. "Ms. Whittaker also told me your workers knew about your invention, and the deals, and have shares. It appears I'm the only one without any share in it at all." She wrapped her arms around her waist and seemed to shrink inside herself.

Dear God. Matt's stomach churned. Could this get any worse?

"Who else knows about you and Elise?" she said softly, her voice filled with a world of pain. "Who else knows about the contracts? How much time were you spending with her when you weren't with me?"

From a faded flower, she'd become like a kicked puppy—a woman thinking she was scorned. Oh, God help him, what to say? How to make this right? "Julie, I've done nothing to earn this level of distrust from you. Okay, so I've spent some time with Elise over the past few months," he admitted, thinking of the days and nights in Elise's company, "but it was purely business." His chin kicked up. "I don't want her, Jules, and she doesn't want me—not anymore."

"Any more?" she pounced on his words. "I thought you said it was only ever friendship."

He resisted the impulse to close his eyes. "Look, I don't know why, but I couldn't feel anything deeper for her—and if she had feelings for me for a little while, friendship is all we feel now. When I told her about you, she was happy for me, for us. We decided we would always have been better as friends. I haven't touched her from that day—except a hug or two of jubilation when the water converter worked."

She whitened further, and he could have shoved a gym bag full of dirty socks in his stupid mouth for saying that. Hadn't he learned the lesson yet? *Never give away too much, son.*

Women only want to know enough to make them happy.

He reached for her. "I don't even know why we're having this conversation. Everything I've done, I've done for us—for our future."

She moved away, shaking her head. "Future?" she whispered. "A future of what, Matt? More secrets? More months and years in which you do these amazing things, and your mother, your ex and your workers share your life and I know nothing about it?"

Anger began to surge through him. "Tonight was our engagement party. I did all this for you. What else do I have to do to prove you're the only one for me? You must know that by now."

She moved out of his touch and spoke so softly he could barely hear her. "It seems there's a lot I don't know."

Matt turned her around and looked into her eyes. "Maybe I made a mistake in waiting until tonight to tell you everything at once—but we're getting married, Jules. You either trust me by now or you don't."

She just looked at him with deep, unblinking eyes, but he could see she wasn't truly with him. She'd slipped into the past, remembering another man, an unfaithful man who'd said the same thing.

He didn't have a chance in hell, unless he took control right now.

Taking her hands in his, he looked into her eyes and said, with what he hoped was quiet strength, "Sit down and listen to me, Jules, and I'll tell you everything. I was going to tell you tonight, anyway. I'd planned it all."

"You mean there's more?" she whispered, sounding horrified. "Not…not now, Matt. No more now…"

One look at her white face and dilated eyes told him what he'd done to her. He knew there was no way he could tell her his final secret tonight, he couldn't let her down again. It would break her.

There was only one thing he could think to say. "I love you, Jules."

She didn't answer in words; she even refused to look at him now. Finally, after what seemed hours, she spoke. "I don't know you…"

He couldn't speak, couldn't think, couldn't even *breathe*. He was about to lose the love of his life because of a damned reporter!

When she spoke, it had nothing to do with what he'd just said. Or maybe it did. "Thank you for making me feel like a queen tonight." She looked up then, and he saw her eyes glimmering with tears. She kissed his cheek, and it froze him through with its gentle good manners and definite farewell. "Spend time with your mother while she's here. Tell her about your inventions, and the deals you're making. Or you can talk to Elise. She seems a lovely person, and wouldn't just accept 'it's only work, I wouldn't want to bore you with the technical details.'"

He might have been angered further still by her mirroring of his words if he hadn't heard the truth inside them…that he'd done more than merely hurt her by his months of silence. The slight hiccupping rasp at the end of each sentence was a sure sign Jules was close to tears, if she wasn't crying already.

Though emotional by nature, Julie never cried for effect. She didn't know how to manipulate him. She was crystal clear, impulsive and giving, funny and adorable—

And walking out the door.

He ran after her. "Julie, I won't let you leave now, not like this. We have to talk."

She kept walking. "I can't take any more tonight."

He grabbed her by the wrist to stop her walking out, but she pushed at him with her free hand. "I need time, Matt. You gave me the night of my life—the best and the worst. I'm feeling pretty betrayed right about now. I need to get my head around it."

Shock held him immobile, rendered him speechless. As death knells to love went, *betrayed* ranked among the worst words.

And then she was gone.

He was wrenching her car door open before he knew he'd followed her. "Don't do this to us, Julie! Damn it, Elise is only a friend—she was only ever a friend. I never loved her. She knows that. Ask her! I love you, only you!"

She stared up at him and hiccuped again. "How can you love me, if you don't trust me with your life?"

God help me. "It wasn't like that. Please don't go, Jules. Stay. Talk to me," he said, dropping his voice for the last sentence, suddenly conscious of his mother in the house behind them.

But the tears streaming down Julie's face told him that talking was the last thing she wanted to do now. At least with him.

Gently, with finality, she closed the car door to her little compact and drove away. No wrenching gears, no racing out. She just left.

She left, and Matt stood there staring after her, reading his future in the past fifteen minutes and without a single clue what to do about it.

CHAPTER TWO

Eight Weeks Later

NEVER in his life had Matt thought he'd be reduced to fighting this dirty. But here he stood outside The Wedding Belles, Julie's place of work, ready to—

Stop thinking about it. Just do it.

Standing next to his car, Matt tightened his jaw and flipped open his phone. "Hey, Callie, I'm outside. Is everything ready?"

"All systems up and running," The Wedding Belles' florist, Callie, replied, with a low laugh. Then, after a short silence, she whispered, "I'm used to doing… unusual things, and this has to be the most romantic way I've ever helped out a friend. But are you sure about this? This really is a federal offence."

"Not if she's willing, and since she's my fiancée, I think we can assume she will be," he replied lightly enough to reassure Callie. But inside, the gripping of his stomach, clenching over and over, signaled his desperation. Would Julie be willing once she knew what this was really about?

He'd pushed her to the edge over the past few months, been a fool to keep so many secrets from her—but he knew this one last secret could destroy them. He'd been trying to tell her for weeks, but after the night of their engagement party, even the thought of telling her made him freeze inside. His tongue glued to his mouth, he retreated behind his old friend and ally, silence.

A real man bears his burdens and mistakes alone. And he puts them right alone. His grandfather's words.

After everything he'd put her through, to tell her now could be the end of them. But damn it, he wouldn't *let* her walk out on him. Whatever it took, he'd keep her with him.

Callie's voice started him out of his morbid thoughts. "Personally, I love what you're doing. I wish Jared had thought about doing this to me," she laughed, "but a couple of the girls are scared about becoming accessories to some kind of felony. And Jared's worried, too."

He didn't blame Callie's husband…in fact,

he couldn't blame any of them. "I won't force her into anything she doesn't want to do," he said. But it was the biggest lie he'd ever told. He'd keep her in the car, in his house, in his life. Whatever it took to win her, he'd do it, short of a real abduction. He wasn't *that* crazy.

He was just a man about to lose the woman he adored with a dozen words, and desperate enough to take the biggest risk of his life.

He'd spent a score of sleepless nights during the past eight weeks since the engagement-party disaster, trying to pull a rabbit out of a hat, searching for the elusive miracle that would allow him to tell her what he should have told her at the start. But he'd been so lost in the happiness he'd never known before meeting Julie that the right time and the right words had never come.

Now it was too late.

At exactly 4:47 this morning, as the first threads of dawn had stretched their fingers across the sky, he'd squared his shoulders and faced the fact that he'd screwed up. Big-time. He should have told her about this long before he'd asked her to marry him, even before he'd found out McLachlan's was in trouble. Now she didn't want to know.

He'd thought giving her time would help. He'd crossed the country on a six-week nonstop selling tour after the fatal night of the engagement party, showing off the land prototype of his converter, and had sold its practical applications to two major players. Finally McLachlan's was safe for future generations. Now his mother could have the comfortable retirement she deserved…and his workers and their families were secure.

He was finally free to tell Julie everything—to make her hear it. He'd been coming over to The Wedding Belles', to her office apartment, and calling every day, from wherever he'd been—but she was now the one fobbing him off. She'd been avoiding him since the night of the party, and was using his own defence of "Don't worry, it's just work" against him.

The games would stop today. Julie would forgive him when she knew the truth. He refused to accept anything less. She was his life blood, his soul, and he'd fight for what was his. The rest of the plans he'd made with The Belles—the changes for their wedding—would prove that to Julie, when she was ready to hear them.

Hiding the grim resolution, he said to Callie, "So send her out. Let Julie's kidnapping begin!"

Surely every bride feels this same need to bolt as the wedding gets close….

But Julie knew the stats. She'd reassured hundreds of nervous grooms, but only a few nervous brides in the three years she'd been working at The Wedding Belles.

What was *wrong* with her? She had everything—a dream wedding, Mr. Right…

Or so she'd thought, and that was the trouble. Since the night of their engagement party, she'd begun to wonder if he'd ever loved her, or if he was merely doing the right thing, the *gentlemanly* thing, rewarding her for standing by him during the dark times for McLachlan's.

She knew it was paranoid, but whenever he was in town and came to see her, or when he called, she could hear it—he had something he needed to tell her, but it was bad. His obvious unhappiness at needing to tell her spoke for itself.

He'd been distracted for weeks before the party. She'd thought it was to do with the creation and marketing of the water converter that not only saved McLachlan's but made him rich again.

Matt and *Elise*, that was.

She couldn't face him. Couldn't let him touch her. She'd never been able to resist him when his hands were on her, and there were too many doubts…not to mention that the wedding had become bigger than either of them. It resembled a runaway train careering downhill at a breakneck pace, and gaining speed by the second.

"Am I missing something, or has the hallway become more fascinating than it was half an hour ago?"

Julie smiled at Callie, the cheeky Belle. She used to use humour to hide her emotions from others; now, ecstatically wed to her high-school buddy turned sweetheart, Jared, whom they'd dubbed "My Favourite Geek", Callie used humour to dig.

"Uniformity can be a good thing now and then," she quipped back, hoping the joke didn't fall flat. Hoping Callie didn't keep digging. Her friends had all been trying to get her to talk to them for weeks now—since a few days after the engagement party—and it was obvious she was tense whenever she had to be with Matt for another interview or photo shoot. It was so *tiring* trying to act the happy bride-to-be, especially when every other Belle *was* a happy new bride or bride-to-be—or ecstatic new wife, in Regina's case.

But until she'd spoken to Matt, it would be a betrayal.

The trouble was what to say. Three months

ago she'd been certain Matt was the love of her life. Now she didn't feel sure of anything.

"Change can be even better." Callie said, braking in on Julie's gloomy thoughts with a mysterious air...and a little wink.

Julie stared at her. "What's that supposed to mean?"

Callie shrugged just as Regina and Serena came out of their respective offices, and with conspiratorial smiles, each took one of Julie's arms. "All work and no play has made Julie a very uptight girl lately. It's time you had some fun."

"And we know just the man you should be having fun with..." Regina said, with a mock-demure air.

Natalie and Audra joined the others. Since there were no arms left to take, Audra loosened Julie's hair from its tight braid—her latest attempt to tame her wretched red curls—and Natalie put her hand firmly between Julie's shoulder blades, pushing her toward the entryway.

"What have you done?" Julie asked, torn between laughter, dread and a sudden sense of gladness, a soaring *hope*.

Stupid woman. What are you expecting, hoping for?

Serena, another ecstatic newlywed, laughed. "We're merely walking you out the door, darling. Welcome to your kidnapping. You're off to the airport. He arranged everything, and you'd better go along with it!"

Matt had done this? What had he arranged…? Julie's heartbeat fluttered as anticipation took wings. Was this what they needed? What had he arranged? Flowers perhaps, champagne, an island in the Caribbean? A week or two of the romance that had been stolen from them during the near collapse of McLachlan Industries, and the high-society, very public cancellation that had almost destroyed The Wedding Belles…?

Just an opportunity to talk—

What do we talk about? The secrets he'd been keeping? Elise?

Sudden panic gripped her. She didn't know if she was ready to hear what he had to say. She tried to gather her thoughts, marshal arguments, but all she could think was time alone for the first time in a long time…with *Matt*. "But…my desk…"

"Is manned adequately and doin' just fine, darlin'," came the ladylike twang of the original Belle. "I haven't done this in a long while. It'll be fun. You've been a rock here since things started going downhill with the Vandiver cancellation. It's our turn to give to you. You officially have two weeks off."

"I already have next month off for the wedding and honeymoon," she protested, feeling her throat closing up in protest and her heart, her stupid heart doing double time, whispering, *Matt, Matt...*

"We know," Regina said gently, and kissed her cheek. "Consider this our prewedding present to you. You've covered for us during the past few months while we've fallen in love, beaten you to the altar or reconciled." She smiled with quiet happiness, and Julie tried hard not to feel eaten up with envy, knowing each of the Belles deserved what they had. "And you never once complained."

"So go." Belle waved a hand with the Southern grace that allowed no room for dissent. "Get out that door, feel the sunshine and wind on your face and enjoy some time with that good-looking young man of yours."

"It was *your* love story that helped us all find ours," Callie said softly as they all marched her down the front passageway to the outside door. "We owe you, girl, big-time. Nobody deserves some happy time more than you and Matt. Now go."

They pushed her gently through to the front of the building that housed The Wedding Belles. And beside the simple sedan he'd bought when he'd sold his beloved Jaguar to pay for her engagement ring, stood a tall, dark-haired man with touches of grey threaded through it, eyes like Antarctic ice, and a mouth so beautifully formed, so *male*, she ached to kiss him, long, slow and hot, until the fire blasted to life and she forgot the world existed.

Just as always.

The man of her daydreams, and more recently, her day-nightmares. *Matt.*

And, just like her daydream, he had flowers in one hand—but though he grinned and winked at the Belles, it was the expression hiding in his eyes that caught her breath in her throat. Bleak. Haunted. Resolute.

Nothing had changed.

It was time…and she definitely wasn't ready to hear what he had to say.

After Matt handed Julie into the car with his customary courtesy, the remaining Belles sighed and looked at each other with a mixture of uneasiness and determination.

"I hope we did the right thing," Natalie said quietly.

All of the Belles nodded. Not one of them had been truly fooled by Matt's "kidnap" plan. Things had been strained between Julie and

Matt for too long to be fixed with a quick romantic getaway, and Matt was far from stupid.

And they, too, had seen the look in his eyes.

Callie bit her lip. "I know how it feels to be with the wrong man. What if we just helped push Julie the wrong way?"

Audra sighed and looked bleak. Serena frowned, shading her eyes as she gazed after the departing car. "No. She loves Matt. I know she does…"

But her voice lacked its customary briskness and confidence.

Oddly enough, it was Regina, the least confident Belle unless she was behind her camera, who ended the indecision. "If Julie's lost her faith, girls, we have to have it for her. No fears shown. No hesitation or uncertainty. I nearly lost Dell because of a lack of faith. I kept everything a secret, from him more so than from you, but all of you as well."

"Me, too, with Kane," Serena added soberly.

"Pride, fear and embarrassment can be a recipe for disaster," Audra sighed.

"I believe we all met for a reason, and that Julie came to us for a reason. And I believe it's partly because of Julie and Matt that we're all so happy now. It's our turn to give." Regina looked around at each of her dearest friends. "I

think Belle's right. If Julie won't share her
worries with us, then we'll keep throwing her
together with Matt and see what happens. And
believe the best will happen for them both,
because we love them. Now, I don't know about
you girls, but I have a four-thirty about to come
in and I have to turn the studio into a Carnivale
in fourteen and a half minutes."

The others smiled at Regina, still with the
same uneasiness, but turned and walked into the
building.

He was about to lose the entire contents of his
stomach. Or maybe it was his heart that was
coming up. It sure felt as if it was in his
mouth about now.

Despite his plans to win her over, all the things
he'd worked out to say, he barely spoke until he
took the turnoff to the airport. He couldn't make
the words form. All he could think to say was,
Do you still love me? But how could he, when
he was almost sure he knew the answer and there
was no way in hell he was prepared to hear it?

The clock was ticking. He had less than ninety
minutes left to tell her, and trust that she'd be the
strong, understanding woman he'd fallen in love
with. The woman he'd relied on through the
worst time of his life. His beautiful Julie…

"So," she said, holding her flowers with fingers about to snap the stems, her voice over-bright. "The girls said we're going to the airport. I hope you had things packed for me? Where are we heading—skiing? The Caribbean islands?" The final two words bordered on sarcastic. Obviously, his silence had given away that this wasn't the kind of surprise it seemed.

She'd given him the opening he needed, but he refused to jump in and say it, to shock her that way. "Jules, you know I've been trying to get you alone since the day after our engagement party. I need to tell you something important, but you've been—" he paused so she'd get the full sense of his meaning "—very busy. But I knew you wouldn't say no to the Belles if they helped me arrange time off for you."

She flushed, as he'd expected she would. Julie's honesty compelled her to say what came next. "I know it seems like I've been avoiding you…"

"Seems like?" He heard the rip-roaring fury in his voice, and knew it came from months of hurt. "You *have* avoided me, for almost two months now. You don't call me or come to see me. When we have to be together, you only touch me in front of the cameras or to reassure your friends." He held up a hand as she began to speak, her face filled with weary resentment. "And I'm sick to death of hearing that it's the job. I see the other Belles spending time with their men, so stop making excuses."

"So you're more intelligent than me," she snapped. "I believed your excuses for months on end. And your work never came in a prettier package than Elise."

He refused to dignify that with a retort. Surely she must know he'd been faithful to her! Her problem had come from finding out about his work arrangements from a stranger. "You're right about my making excuses. I have done that, but not for the reasons you think." Once he'd turned onto the freeway leading to Logan International Airport, he said, "Time's run out, Julie. It's time for us to be honest—both of us."

Beside him, he felt her freeze. "So, I gather this isn't the romantic getaway the girls believed it was when they helped you?"

"No." He kept his gaze on traffic. "But you already knew that."

"So you lied to them, to our friends?"

He shrugged. "They drew their own conclusions. I didn't correct them."

"Sliding out of the truth is lying in my book," she said, her tone left sarcasm behind, and headed straight into belligerence.

You ought to know, you've been doing it for months, he almost said; but an innate sense of honesty made him admit she was right: she'd only followed his example.

She'd been flashing her anger as bright as sunlight. She didn't want to hear what he had to say. She didn't want to know. Avoiding him had been all she could do to stop this final confrontation from happening—and time was up. Luring him into a fight was her last stand against the end.

"It wasn't their place to know, Julie. I had to tell you first. After today, everyone will know anyway."

The blood drained from her face, making her freckles stand out in sharper contrast. "I see," she whispered. Her head lowered to where her thumbnails scratched at her index fingers. One of a legion of nervous habits he'd learned to read: she was nervous as hell and hiding it with belligerence.

But why? Why didn't she take the opening he'd given her, and ask him to stop the car so she could get out, or just throw the ring back in his face?

The Belles. She's staying in this engagement for her friends' sake.

Since the Vandiver cancellation, the mammoth event that had gone belly-up without payment, the whole business had been on the rocks. Proud and fiercely independent, the women of The Wedding Belles wouldn't take a cent from their men to stay afloat. But when it had hit the media rounds that The Belles, in debt themselves, were giving Julie and Matt the best wedding they could afford, Julie Montgomery and Matt McLachlan were suddenly hailed as the love match of the year, and the Belles as "wedding planners with heart." Since then, brides and their mothers had flocked to The Wedding Belles to book their weddings…but, as ever with this kind of business, payments were slow to come in. They couldn't afford a single cancellation now.

The Belles couldn't afford to lose the McLachlan-Montgomery wedding.

He couldn't be angry with her for caring about her friends, no matter how it hurt, no matter how damn *rejected* he felt, how alone in a love story he'd believed was forever.

What he had to say, to ask, was far too important to blurt out in anger, or in retaliation for whatever she threw at him. Given what he'd put her through, he deserved it.

"You haven't asked why we're headed to the airport," he said abruptly.

Her mouth was half-open, ready for a retort, but then it closed. As she thought, her lower lip pushed out, almost like pouting but far sexier because it was natural. Like her sensuality, it was so much a part of her she didn't think about it.

Suddenly his body reminded him that it had been a long time since she'd shown him the full extent of that loving sensuality. He ached with the need for her touch, for the beauty of their union—and even more he ached for the connection that, to him, meant he'd found his one and only, the commitment to forever he'd made in his heart the night she'd said the words he'd cherish all his life. "All I want is you."

A shaft of pain pierced him like a gunshot, as he thought of the way she'd loved him right from the moment she'd tripped and landed at his feet the first day. She'd looked up, laughing at her clumsiness, willing to share the joke against herself in a way he'd come to know was uniquely Julie. Then the look in her eyes turned to wonder as she saw him. "Here's my number," she'd said within a minute in that adorable accent of hers, writing with a permanent marker on his hand. "And here're my lips," she'd whispered when she'd finished writing. She'd kissed him with a sweetness and desire he'd never known in his life. It was so amazing he'd forgotten they were in the middle of a milling crowd on a busy city street. He'd forgotten he was in a convenient, please-the-parents relationship with Elise, and he'd vowed never to cheat on a woman in his life. He hadn't been able to think beyond the moment, the woman whose name he hadn't even known. He'd drawn her into his arms and kissed her right back.

She hadn't known his name, either. For the first time a woman hadn't known he was Matthew McLachlan of McLachlan Marine Industries, one of Boston's most eligible bachelors. And when on their second date he'd told her, she'd said, "Oh?", with a semblance of polite interest when she so obviously didn't care that it had made him laugh out loud, something he'd rarely done in his lifetime. "So does that mean I don't have to worry about how you're going to pay for dinner?"

And she'd stood by him after his father's sudden death eight weeks later, and he'd discovered how deep the problems at McLachlan's ran. The mess in which his father had left the business with schemes and investments that had failed time after time.

"I never had wealth in my life to care about, Matt," she'd said, holding him close. "I care if it hurts you—but whether you want to save the business or you want to start over—no matter what, I'll still be here." And then she'd said those beautiful words he'd never forget. "All I want is you."

He was about to test "no matter what," and "all I want is you" to their limits. Would she still be here tomorrow? Would he still be all she wanted? Would she want him at all?

"So, why are we going to the airport?"

In their fourteen months together, he'd never heard such a distant tone from her.

He exited onto the airport turnoff. They were almost there. He swallowed the bitter bile rising in his throat and said the words he'd rehearsed ever since he'd recruited The Belles to help him "kidnap" her. "I realise this is terrible timing. I wouldn't blame you if you never want to see me again. But I'm asking you not to walk away, not today. I need you, Julie."

After a few moments, she asked, simply, "Why?"

There was nothing else to do but blurt it out. "My ex, Kirsten, was married on Saturday—"

"You…you were married?" The shock, the pain of quick jealousy in her voice made him want to hit himself, and yet a small part of him rejoiced. What a stupid jerk to shock her like that—but she wouldn't feel any pain, surely, unless she still cared?

"No," he was quick to reassure her. "We never married. Kirsten's my ex-girlfriend. But that isn't the point. We had—have a child together. Molly's seven, and she's on her way to stay with me for two weeks while Kirsten and Dan are on their honeymoon. Her plane lands in an hour."

CHAPTER THREE

ONE moment passed, then two, before Julie made a small, choking sound, then another and another. "You…you…?" Further words were impossible, as she doubled over herself, coughing and spluttering.

But as she choked on her words, she couldn't stop them going round and round in her head. *He has a daughter?*

She must have spoken them aloud at some point, for he answered in a restrained, polite tone that made her long to biff him over the head. "Yes. I should have told you about Molly long ago. I didn't. There's no excuse I can give you."

Somehow she found her voice, even if it came out as a croak half-lost in a cough. "Just like that?" The words came out strangled as she coughed again and again, choking on saliva.

He must have pulled the car over sometime

in the past minute, because she felt the stillness around her, and a gentle hand patting her back. He didn't speak until her fit subsided. "What do you want me to say?"

"Maybe an apology, an excuse, a reason?" was all she managed in reply.

He frowned at her, as if she'd said something stupid. "What reason could I have? What excuse would work? Would an apology help you feel better, or make me any less of a jerk for not telling you about Molly before?"

Strangely his admission that he'd acted badly only made her angrier with him. "Maybe not—though it might have helped to have had some preparation time to meet her, say, a bit more than an hour?" She coughed a final few times and finally felt clear—at least in her throat and lungs. "You're right, nothing could make you less of a jerk now, but it doesn't mean I don't deserve an apology, does it?"

"No. I should have told you earlier, Julie. I'm sorry."

She kept her gaze on her hands, formed into fists on her lap. She mumbled, "Of course you are. Such a gentleman." The words sounded sarcastic, even to her ears. She'd expected the words—but right now, she didn't feel like forgiving him.

As if in echo of her thoughts, he said, "Don't think it, Julie. Say it. Say what you're feeling, about Molly—and about me."

That was the trouble. There were too many things she wanted to say, to ask. Would he know the answers? Did she want to hear them?

Suddenly she felt tired of living in this limbo. She hated feeling so cold, so numb inside, filled with fear and regret, not knowing what was going on between them or why. Even the shock running through her veins was better than the nothingness. It was time. She had to know.

"Is that where you went when you flew out of Boston those few times, and didn't want me to come?"

He nodded. "I don't see enough of Molly, but I fly down to spend time with her whenever I can. I want her to know who her father is, that I care about her. I want her to be sure her dad didn't just abandon her."

Filled with the strangest mixture of fury, betrayal and relief, she turned away. Glad to just *feel,* words slipped out she never meant to speak. "I wondered, especially the fourth time two months back…"

A short silence. "You thought I had another woman?" He spoke slowly, as if he'd just come to the realisation. The shock in his voice was clear.

She noticed her thumbnail was in her mouth. Chewing her nails under stress was a habit she thought she'd broken when she was seventeen. Pulling it out, she made herself shrug. "What would you have thought had it been *me* taking off for parts unknown, making obvious excuses for you not to come—especially when you went just ten days before the party? What would you think if I had a male working partner—an ex-lover, no less—and I'd disappeared for a week just before our engagement party?"

After another long stretch of quiet, he answered in a curt tone. "Maybe I'd have thought the same things you obviously did—but I would have asked you about it. *If* I was given a chance to see you alone, or you allowed me to speak to you, that is." No longer polite, his voice sounded cold, furious.

"So *if* you'd seen me alone in the past ten months—since you started disappearing without explanation—and I'd asked if you had another lover, would you have told me about your daughter?" she challenged, turning to face him with a fury to match his. "You wouldn't have said 'it's just work' again? You might have actually trusted me with something about your life the magazines don't know?"

His jaw tightened. "You've thought that for ten months?"

She sighed. "You should know I would never have become your lover, let alone become engaged to you, if I'd thought it back then."

He was pale, his face remote, untouchable. "Well, you should know I don't cheat. I've never cheated on a woman in my life. Except the day you kissed me," he finished with a hard irony that made her feel…feel—"and I went straight to her and told her I'd met you, and ended it. After fourteen months together, you should know better than to accuse me of that. Sneaking around behind someone's back, saying one thing to one woman and promising the other something else, lying and manipulating and hurting everyone is the act of a selfish loser and pathetic coward."

There was no way he was lying; but the fury in his eyes—the shadows of something in the past—told her this was a wound he wouldn't let her touch.

Another door he'd closed in her face.

"I went to see Molly that time because she called to tell me about her mom getting married. It sounded like she needed me," he informed her, his tone, so restrained and polite, hitting her like a whiplash. "But it was only a week before our engagement party, and it seemed the wrong time to tell you I have a daughter. But right now it feels as if any time would have been a bad time. If you can't believe I was faithful to you, I was always going to be in the wrong, no matter what I did."

She felt the heat stain her cheeks, an unspoken acknowledgement that he was right—but it only made her angrier. He had no *right* to be right…correct—oh, to *hell* with semantics! He had to be in the wrong now!

"So you think I wouldn't have understood if you'd told me at the start of our relationship?" she challenged. "Why was it a bad time then? Was it always going to be a bad time to tell me?" A shaft of uncertainty lanced through her. "Am I so hard to confide in? Am I so…so non-understanding? Why was it so intimidating to tell me about Molly?" *Or about anything else, it seems…*

He shook his head and sighed. "It wasn't like that. You have your ways of making it hard to confide, but not in the way you mean."

"I see," she whispered, looking at her hands again.

"No, I don't think you do." His hands gripped

the steering wheel. His face was pale and set, looking forward, out to the passing traffic. Shutting another door in her face. Making it impossible to ask what he meant.

"Does Molly know about me? That you have a fiancée?" she asked after a while, but knew the answer before it came.

"Not yet." Again, no apology. No excuse.

Rebellion rose higher in her throat. She wanted the truth. She *needed* to hear the answers. She had to know. And she wanted to deck him!

But did she hit first or ask first? She was too *furious* to ask the question that had been hovering in her mind for months. Why should she ask if he'd ever loved her in truth, or was marrying her to avoid public humiliation on both their parts? He'd only give the perfect reassurance. And he might even believe it was the truth…but *she* wouldn't believe it. She wasn't the trusting fool she'd been a few months ago.

"I don't know you," she finally said, and felt a massive sense of relief fill her. That was it, exactly what worried her the most. Worse still, the anger that had sustained her over the past few minutes was fading, leaving her vulnerable. She couldn't attack him, couldn't maintain the emotion that kept a distance from him. Truth was all she had left.

The cool, well-bred look disappeared from his face. "What?" His voice rang with disbelief.

"I don't know you." She wanted to look away, to put up a barrier against the utter stupidity of the situation, but she forced herself to keep looking at him. "I don't think I ever did."

The bewilderment in his eyes told her that it was the last thing he'd expected to hear from her. "How can you say that? You know me better than anyone."

She shook her head, seeing he honestly believed it. "Tell me how I know you that well—or at all—when you've never told me anything that was close to your heart."

His jaw clenched shut. His eyes were hard chips of ice. It was obvious he wasn't going to answer, if he had an answer to give.

She sighed. "We've been together fourteen months, engaged for five months, and you never told me about your daughter. You never told her about me. What does that say about how much you trust me? If you can't tell your daughter about me until the day I'm going to meet her, four weeks before our wedding, what does it say about how much you love and trust me?"

His hands gripped the steering wheel until the knuckles showed white. "It wasn't like that. You're misinterpreting—"

"How else could I interpret it?" Suddenly she was fighting tears. "The omissions—all of them—speak more than a thousand words. I'm good enough to take to bed, to get a ring and pretty words, but you didn't tell me one of the most treasured parts of your life. You didn't want me to meet your own child." She bit her lip but said it. "You don't love me, Matt. I don't think you ever did."

A long silence, so dark it touched her heart, wounded her like a knife. "This has nothing to do with how I feel for you. Not all families are close, or treasure each other as yours does, Julie."

She'd already known that. She was blessed to have brothers and sisters who loved as much as they teased her, a mother who loved her kids dearly but never withheld things from them they needed to know, and a father who knew how to hug his kids, how to talk to them, to want to know what was going on in their lives and what they needed.

Matt and his mother were very close, but his well-bred, highly demanding, now dead father had left scars on Matt's emotions she could see, though he'd never talked about them. She'd believed, *hoped,* he'd tell her, one day.

Now she doubted he ever would—and she couldn't live this way.

"Your secrecy about your daughter isn't the point. It's only the final symptom." She swallowed hard, bit her lip, but the stinging behind her eyes told her she was about to lose control. "There's almost nothing about my life and past you don't know. I trusted you with everything, good, bad or humiliating." She drew a shaking breath. "But you've locked me out of what's most important to you. You gave me beautiful words, but never shared your worries, your fears or burdens about McLachlan's. You sold the Jaguar and bought me an exquisite ring without discussing it with me, even though it was *for* me." Searching for words, she shrugged as she went on, her voice scratchy. "You've given no input into our wedding. You just showed up for photos, or smiled and said, 'Whatever you want is fine.' I never know what you want, or if you hate everything. You never told me anything about your invention, or working with Elise. You couldn't even tell me you had a daughter you needed to visit." Tears rushed up so hard and fast her eyes burned. "I don't know you because you don't let me in." She turned from him, so he wouldn't see how much the admission hurt her.

Matt closed his eyes and let his mind speak a quick, fervent prayer, but he knew he was on his own with this. He'd been prepared for fury, a fight, his ring handed back or thrown back in his face. But this bewildered betrayal, the tears Julie could never put on for show, shocked him to the core almost as much as the words she'd spoken.

Perhaps because they were a mirror of her words two months ago—and what she hadn't said then, she said now. She hadn't said she didn't love him, but that he didn't love her. She hadn't said it was over; she'd said she didn't *know* him. That he hadn't made her a real and true part of his life.

How could he argue? It wasn't the truth from his point of view, but it all made horrible sense from hers.

"I didn't tell you about my work because you were going through so much with The Wedding Belles." His throat felt thick and hot, his voice raw and hurting. "I wanted to protect you."

She wouldn't look at him. "Protecting me or locking me out. It's all the same in the end. I know nothing about your world, your life."

He gulped down a word a McLachlan would never say, but oh, how he wanted to right now. "When I sold the car to buy your ring, I didn't say anything because I wanted to give you a lovely surprise. The ring in the glass, etcetera."

"But we talked about that, long before the night we became engaged. We agreed that since we loved each other, every choice we made should be a joint decision." Her words, her tone, gave no quarter. "It ought to have been our choice, but you took that away from me. I would have been happy with anything we could afford. Sacrifices like that shouldn't be made or decided alone." He felt her gaze on him as she said, "You agreed to it."

"And you're letting my mistake come between us," he said. "You're putting up walls between us for one error in judgment?"

"Mistake? *One* error?" she echoed, then gave a hollow laugh. "Which one, Matt? We haven't even started yet. There're a few to go—like why you never told me about the water converter or Elise." She sucked in a breath. "I think I need to know now."

Matt would have liked to have breathed, too, but there suddenly wasn't enough air in the car. He felt as if he was being smothered slowly. "Not telling you about the water converter before its success was—it was just a man thing, Julie." He shrugged mentally and thought, *What the hell? I may as well tell her the lot.* "You're not an engineer. I didn't think you'd understand the applications any more than I'd understand how to put a wedding together—and I didn't have the time or energy then to explain it all."

"Did you ever give me a chance to understand, either the converter or the partnership?" she asked quietly. "Did you ever say, 'Sorry, Julie, I'm inventing something that could revolution-ise the industry and save the company. I might be a bit distracted while I'm doing that—and it has nothing to do with the beautiful ex-girlfriend that I happen to be working with, by the way'?"

"We both know I didn't," he snapped, furious more with himself than her, but did she have to tear down all his reasons and make him look like such a jerk?

"While you're putting the rope around my neck, I might as well be hanged and be done with it," he said wearily, refusing to tell her how much damn *input* he'd had into their wedding lately. He didn't think she'd even care at this point. "I didn't have input into the wedding because I didn't give a damn if we wore ten-thousand-dollar outfits in a cathedral or day clothes in the city hall, I just wanted to marry you."

"While you're being hanged, why not be honest about it?" she retorted, just as tired. "Tell the whole truth, Matt, not just the part that makes you look good."

He wound down the window and sucked in the streaming air, filled with car exhaust. "Fine. I was busy trying to save the business, and I was grateful you and your friends were handling everything so well. All I had to do was show up, smile and cuddle or kiss you for photos."

"And that's exactly what I saw. A man who couldn't care less about our big day."

"Yes, all right, I was busy trying to save the family business. It was wrong, giving you the burden of it—but all I wanted was to marry you. I didn't care about the finer details. For heaven's sake, you're the wedding planner. Most guys leave the wedding stuff to the women." Seeing the stubbornness radiating from her still, he snapped, "Don't you get it, Julie? I went along with your friends' plans because I wanted to give you everything you wanted. All I wanted was you," he mimicked her words, the words he'd treasured for so long, with obvious bitterness.

"Tell that to the press, Matt, because I can't believe it. Not anymore."

He was almost reeling by now with the effects of one attack after another...and yes, all warranted, damn it. And it still hadn't finished; she'd barely dealt with his partnership with Elise.

Not telling her about Elise had been a no-brainer. He'd waited until the partnership was only financial, because then Julie would be able see it from a past perspective. Over and done with, and he was ready to devote his life, time and future to her alone.

But telling her that was as futile as it was impossible. She refused to believe him. She didn't even believe he loved her. He might as well tell her why he hadn't talked about Molly and have it over with.

The reason sickened him, it might as well sicken her, too, and be the last gasp for his dying love story.

"I didn't tell you about Molly because it shows me up as an uncaring jerk and the bad father I am," he said bluntly.

Julie gasped, and for once, seemed to have nothing to say. And for some reason, that sent a small eddy of hope streaming into the emotional storm he was wading through.

Suddenly Julie's words from their first date came back to him, when she'd almost stepped into a puddle of slush.

"Don't protect me, Matt," she'd said. "Life's an adventure. Let it happen, even if I end up falling on my face. You never know—I might even let you come along for the ride. I promise it'll be fun," she'd added, with a grin and a wink, and that look in her eyes that begged, demanded another kiss.

At that moment he'd known he was in love for life. He adored her life philosophy almost as much as he adored her—because Julie, open-hearted, frank, chatty, laughing Julie was everything he wasn't.

All his life Matt had been trained not to speak unless spoken to, never to jump in with explanations but to rehearse them, to always consider his words before he spoke. To "A McLachlan," making a fool of one's self was the ultimate anathema. One spoke of love in the darkness of the bedroom, or at appropriately quiet times. One touched the woman one loved only when alone. One apologised with dignity. One must always be conscious of one's position in life.

And this one had been *bored* all his life until an adorable red-haired dynamo had fallen at his feet and laughed about it. She laughed about everything, especially herself. She had a habit of blurting out whatever was on her mind, talked out all her decisions with him, held his hand and hugged him on their first date. She'd told him she loved him three weeks after they met, and every day from then. And she'd screamed to the room, "We're engaged!" when she'd seen the diamond solitaire floating in her champagne glass at Boston's best restaurant. The whole room had shared her joy, applauding her when she'd held the ring aloft on her finger, dancing across the room and dragging him with her, laughing.

And, most beautiful of all, she made love as if it were the last time she ever would, whispering unashamed words of love, telling him she'd love him all her life.

Or, she *had* talked everything out with him, until it had stopped abruptly, the night of the engagement party. She *had* made love to him until then. She *had* told him she loved him whenever she saw him—until two months ago.

She was going to leave him, and dear God, to have to go back to being "A McLachlan" again, after loving Julie...

No! Damn it, I won't lose you! he wanted to yell.

He'd win her back, even if he had to step in a puddle or fall on his face.

"Kirsten—Molly's mother—didn't say anything when I proposed to her." He stared at his white-knuckled fists gripping the wheel. "She'd said, 'I'm pregnant,' and as soon as I'd got over the shock, I proposed. I had to make it right," he said wryly. "I could only imagine how my father would react if I didn't marry

Kirsten. McLachlans have never bred children outside marriage in six generations. She asked for a while to think about it, and frankly, I was relieved to not see her. But a few weeks later Kirsten sent me a letter, saying she'd met the love of her life and was going to Florida with him. She said I needn't tell anyone about the baby. Nobody needed to know about Molly if I didn't want to acknowledge her."

He watched the cars passing them, hoping Julie would take her cue and speak; but it seemed he hadn't said enough to satisfy her yet. "I didn't hear from Kirsten again until Molly was born. I didn't see my child until she was two months old. I saw her again when she was nearly one." He turned to her then, wondering if, with her close family, she could possibly understand what he was about to say. "Molly called Dan, Kirsten's boyfriend, 'Da-da'. She still calls him Dad now. Molly knows who I am, but Dan is her father in every way that counts. To her, I'm the four- or five-times-a-year guy who takes her to movies, museums, restaurants and parks, gives her presents and goes away again."

In the long silence that followed, he held his peace. There was nothing left to say.

"And you never told me this because…?"

He stared at her in disbelief. Wasn't it obvious? Hadn't he embarrassed himself enough? What did she want from him, blood?

As if she'd read his mind, she thrust out her chin. "Peter Blake."

And as answers went, it was perfect. The infamous Peter story—the boy who'd gone out with Julie, even became her first lover, because he'd wanted to get closer to her beautiful, bubbly, blond sister Veronica—had to have been her life's greatest humiliation. Equal to his Kirsten story, in that they'd both been deserted.

Except that in her story only Peter looks bad. In my scenario I'm the jerk, the fool and a bad father to boot.

Gritting his teeth, because it felt as though Julie the emotional dentist was pulling them one by one, he muttered, "I don't like to talk about Molly."

"Why?"

His breath hissed from between his teeth. "Because I couldn't make Kirsten want to marry me even for our child's sake. Because my only child doesn't want to call me Dad or acknowledge me as her father. She calls me her 'biological parent'." He heard the bitterness in the way Molly introduced him to her friends.

"Is that all?" Julie asked softly.

He frowned at her. He'd just poured out his soul, and she wanted still more?

"Maybe you don't talk about Molly because she makes you feel like a failure, and McLachlans don't fail?"

With the pain of her insight stabbing him, he couldn't answer. It might be true, in part; but if Julie didn't believe he loved *her*, what chance did he have of convincing her he'd die for Molly, the adorable, bad-tempered little rebel who barely knew him?

Today's "kidnap" was probably the worst idea he'd ever thought brilliant. He'd already known that telling Julie about Molly on the way to the airport to pick up the daughter who'd rather eat nails than spend two weeks with him was his punishment for not telling her months ago. But trying to win Julie back with Molly here to highlight his complete lack of parenting skills was the closest to useless task he would perform in his life.

But he would. He'd step in that damned puddle, even fall on his face. He'd grab any option right now that kept her in his life for another hour, another day.

Maybe it had no chance of working. But it was the only plan he had, and he'd stick to it until a better idea presented itself. Julie had two weeks off, and though she didn't know it yet, she was spending every damn hour and minute of it with him.

And with Molly, too, God help him.

God help them all.

CHAPTER FOUR

JULIE had never felt such a welter of confused emotions in so short a time in her life, and that was saying something for a person her siblings Jason, Michael, Scott and Veronica had long ago nicknamed "the emotional girl."

Standing in the public part of the terminal, waiting for Matt to return with Molly, Julie tried to do the centre-and-focus thing her friend Rachel had taught her back in high school when her feelings ran away with her. Slow breathing, pray, think positive thoughts. Deal with one thing at a time and feel the satisfaction before moving on to the next thing.

Are you focussing?

Yes, she was—on fifteen things at once, and all of them filling her with fury and sadness and fear and regret. How on earth she was going to deal with the daughter she'd never known Matt had until exactly one hour and sixteen minutes ago?

A crowded airport terminal probably wasn't the best place to find answers, or search for inner peace.

She looked around at the milling people. Smiling, hugging, so glad to see each other, when all she wanted to do was bolt into one of those taxis outside and run away until she could gather her thoughts.

No, she needed to find forgiveness within herself, feel this crushing load of resentment lift from her shoulders, from her heart. But a big, hurting part of her didn't *want* to forgive Matt. She didn't want to let it go.

Holding on to hurts and resentments the way you do only hurts you, darling, her mother always told her.

Maybe she should talk to the smiling group of orange-robed Hare Krishnas handing out pamphlets and cookbooks over near the taxis. They certainly looked as if they had some secret to share—

"Julie."

Well, there went any chance she had of finding tranquility. After one last, longing look at those smiling people, she turned to the deep, melodious voice with just a hint of wildness beneath, the rough touch that always made her think he should try a career in singing…and it inspired anything but serenity in her.

Like his eyes, as ice blue as the Antarctic shelf, and so beautiful with their thick black lashes they made her ache. When he used to smile at her, when he touched her, she would wonder how a man so beautiful could ever love her.

She wondered it now without the smile or the touch.

"Julie, this is my daughter, Molly. Molly, this is my fiancée, Julie."

Trying to feel anything but this huge, swallowing anger, Julie wrenched her gaze from Matt and dropped it by two feet.

Well, no denying whose child she was. Molly was an absolute mini-me of Matt. Black hair that always looked rumpled, except Molly's was tangled; a mouth so full it was almost sulky—in Molly's case, it *was*; and eyes like the Antarctic shelf.

Eyes filled with anger and disdain swept over Julie. "You're kidding, right? You're gonna marry *that?*" Aggression was in every line of her, from her black jeans and a long-sleeved purple T-shirt with the legend "I Burned Down My Dollhouse" across it in death metal letters, to the pugnacious line of her lower lip.

Obviously Molly was not a polite, dolly-and-tea-parties kind of seven-year-old.

With a sigh, Matt put a hand on his

daughter's shoulder. "Molly, you promised you'd be on your best behaviour," he said quietly.

The little girl's face screwed up. "That was before I saw her. It's bad enough when Mom gets mushy with Dan the Man, but at least he's hot and has a motorbike. You never said you were getting it on with a *red*."

"You will not speak to Julie that way, Molly," Matt said with quiet authority. "It won't get you what you want."

The reaction to this piece of parental discipline was folded arms and a sneer. "Wanna bet?"

Matt's reply held only restraint, and Julie marvelled at his ability to hold his temper when Molly was doing her best to provoke him. "No matter what you do, I won't call your grandmother. You are not going home until the day agreed upon. Is that clear?"

Molly's mouth turned mulish. Obviously Matt had called her bluff, and she didn't like it. "I give you two days."

Molly seemed determined to create a scene right here in the airport—and it was obvious to Julie why Matt had forced her here today, why he'd been desperately trying to tell her about Molly for weeks. She'd never seen a father and child who needed a mediator more.

She held out a hand to the child and smiled. "So, Molly, how was your flight? Did you get a movie? Was it good food or did it suck?" She winked at the girl whose clothes yelled "don't you dare treat me like a little kid."

Molly stared suspiciously at her for a moment. "Are you putting on that voice?"

Glad her accent had distracted Molly from her tantrum, Julie grinned. "Well, maybe I did do it up a bit, though I am Australian. But don't ask me to say 'crikey,'" she laughed. "Since I come from Sydney, and not the Outback, I'd probably screw—um, mess it up."

"Cool! You said 'crikey'!" Molly burst out laughing. "Now say 'g'day'…please," she added, with a swift, long-suffering glance at Matt.

"G'day, mate, how're ya goin'?" she replied in an outrageous Outback accent, with a grin and wink. Her accent was one of the reasons the Belles had hired her in the first place. If customers laughed with her and went through Australianisms, they were less likely to walk out without making a booking of some kind—and they usually demanded Julie assist in some way.

Molly beamed at her before turning back to Matt. "Hey, she's pretty cool for a red." She thrust her bag into her father's hands, then tugged at Julie, dragging her along as if Matt didn't exist. "So what're you doing with *him?*"

"Molly."

Julie felt the child stiffen at the sound of her father's voice, and knew she had to take control. No way was Molly going to give in yet.

One minute in the company of father and daughter told Julie these two were far too alike. Matt wanted Molly to stay, and Molly wanted to be on the next flight home. Both father and daughter were out of their depths, and both had plans to get their way.

It was plain to Julie they'd both go down fighting and would cling to their plans in the face of failure. The only difference was in the execution of their plans. Matt would remain cool, polite, a gentleman to the end. A McLachlan born and bred, he was used to getting his way with good manners and subtle manipulation.

Brought up differently and too young for scruples, Molly would do whatever it took to reach her goal, which was obviously to be on a flight home as soon as possible.

"So did the food suck?" Julie asked again, with a long-suffering air. "I hate plane food. I always want to grab a burger and fries the second I'm off a flight."

Molly's mouth twitched and pouted again. "They gave me *chicken nuggets*. Like I'm a little kid. And pasta, on the side—as if pasta goes with nuggets!"

It seemed that, like her father, Molly knew exactly what she wanted when it came to food—and Julie didn't miss the tiny tremble of the full mouth. Suddenly she looked less like a little hellion and more like a very small child who'd been sent away from everyone she knew and all things familiar and loved. Of course she was taking out her insecurities on the only person she could.

Oh, how she could relate to that. Much as she loved her life here, sometimes the loneliness overwhelmed her. The need to call family without first having to check the international clocks. The ache to see a long-familiar face, or turn the TV on and find an Aussie soap opera, and hear her own accent echoed back at her. She'd been twenty-five when she'd begun her travels alone. Not to mention that she'd travelled half the world by the time she was Molly's age.

This poor little darling needed her—and it wasn't her fault Matt had told her nothing. Julie'd push aside her anger now, for Molly's sake.

"Ah, no wonder you're grumpy," she said cheerfully. "So am I. I didn't bring my lunch today. Matt, we need burgers and fries and we need them now."

Molly's face turned piquant with joy. Just the promise of a burger and fries—food that went together—and she truly looked like the little girl she was. "Oh, *yeah!*"

"Julie, I don't think she should be—" Julie trod backward onto Matt's foot so Molly wouldn't see, and he stopped. "Thinking it over, one cranky, hungry female I could do. Two means it's definitely time for burgers and fries."

Molly turned and grinned. "Cool, thanks, Matt."

"A truly wise man knows when he's outnumbered," Julie added, smiling at him over her shoulder. "I didn't have lunch, either. Trust me, you do *not* want to be locked in a car with two unfed females for an hour."

Matt laughed. "The very thought fills me with terror. So tell me, where can one get a burger and fries around here?"

Molly giggled—and then, just before she looked up at Julie as if she'd found an unexpected savior, she smiled at him, too.

Molly actually smiled at him.

Matt, who was famed for the right words at the right time, was speechless. Seeing his daughter smiling at him, seeing *Julie* smile at him like that, with the playful glint in her eyes and a touch of the gentle, sensual speculation he hadn't seen in months, he wondered if he'd slipped into an alternate universe.

Nothing today had gone as he'd planned... but somehow it was working.

Why, he had no idea. He'd said everything wrong, been a jerk and worse, yet Julie didn't hate him. She was even smiling at him. In seven years he hadn't truly connected with Molly...but put Julie into the equation, and Molly smiled at him, was laughing now—and yet she'd vowed to hate his fiancée from the moment Matt'd told her Julie was waiting to meet her.

And fifteen minutes later, watching them wolfing down dripping, mayonnaise-filled burgers he wouldn't touch, dipping their fries in—his stomach churned—*ice cream,* one indisputable fact lodged in his stunned brain.

Julie seemed to understand his daughter as he never had.

Unbelievably, The Brilliant Plan was working thus far, despite his failures. He didn't care what he had to do: he'd carry out the rest of it and make it work.

Crazy, but it was almost enough to make him re-think destiny, or whatever ridiculous philosophy said he wasn't in control of his life.

He re-thought it again minutes later when Julie took Molly to the little girls' room and came out two minutes later alone.

"Where's Molly?" he asked, his stomach suddenly clenching.

"She said she was coming out to you," Julie replied, her eyes wide and filling with the same dread he was feeling. "Matt…"

Knowing his daughter, he didn't waste time searching the local area for a kid playing hide and seek. He called the police.

"Mr. McLachlan, this is Boston Central Police. We have your daughter here."

Striding from bus stop to train station, still in the vicinity of the burger bar—how the hell had she gotten away from here so fast?—and holding his cell phone to his ear, Matt bolted for his car and hopped in, heading for the city. Trying to control the tremors of fear—Dear God, had she taken a lift from a stranger? Had she?—he stuttered into the phone, "Is she…is she—"

The policewoman's voice softened at the obvious panic in Matt's voice. "She's just fine, sir. We found her trying to board a train to Central Station. She's not happy that her mother won't interrupt her honeymoon to collect her, but she's unhurt."

Matt sagged with relief against the steering wheel. It had been more than two hours. Julie had called in all The Belles to find Molly; apparently even The Belles' current customers were in on the search. He'd roped in workers from McLachlan's. "Thank you so much for your help. I'll be there as soon as I can."

He disconnected the phone. Then, driving off, speed-dialed Julie's number on his hands-free phone as he headed toward the centre of Boston. "She's at the Central Police Station. I'm on my way to get her now."

"Oh, thank God. Is she all right?" Julie cried, with the same panic in her voice he'd felt minutes ago. "Did she…was she…?"

"She's fine. Apparently she's upset that Kirsten won't interrupt her honeymoon to get her, though."

"Oh, I'm so glad she's safe!"

"Me, too—but she has some apologies to make for panicking everyone," he said grimly. "Can you call The Belles, while I call my PA at McLachlan's? I'll take Molly back there as soon as I can."

"Don't be too hard on her," Julie said softly. "She's still so little. Is this the first time she's been away from her mother with you? She's just seen her mother get married, and now you're about to, as well. She's probably scared at all the changes in her world, and hiding it with all this acting out, poor little girl."

It took a few moments for the words to sink in. "Oh, damn. That sounds about right." He thought about it some more. "She never acted out like this when I visited her in Florida, but Kirsten said she's been causing trouble from the moment she found out she was coming to stay with me." He smiled into the phone, grateful yet again for the depth of insight and love that was such an integral part of his fiancée. "So how did you get to be so wise about kids?"

"Not kids, just females." Her voice was warmer than he'd heard it in weeks. "And maybe I can relate a little. I love Boston, but there are times I still feel like a fish out of water. Feeling lost doesn't inspire the best in us females."

There was an unconscious wealth of meaning in that—something he needed to know—but he'd arrived at the police station and didn't have time to sort it out. "I'm at the station. I'll call you when I'm heading toward The Wedding Belles. Can you thank everyone and tell them I'll be there soon?"

"No worries."

Matt smiled to himself, hearing the Aussie

slang she still used now and then after four years away from Sydney—

Using the terms that connected her to home, maybe? Terms that made her feel a little less like that fish out of water…?

Click.

Testing the waters, he shot back Aussie terms he'd heard her use sometimes, "Too right. Taa, mate," and grinned as she burst into laughter. "Was it that bad?"

"Worse!" But her sweet gurgle of laughter was the most beautiful sound he'd heard in months. "'Taa' was right—it means thanks— but 'too right'?" She laughed again. "I'd better call the girls. I'll talk to you soon."

But she sounded more reluctant to break the connection than she had in a long time. Maybe making a fool of oneself wasn't as bad a thing as his father and grandfather had believed it to be.

As Julie would say, "Whatever works."

Matt grinned as he ran up the stairs and into the police station to find his recalcitrant daughter.

Julie watched Molly as the celebration over finding her went on.

Natalie brought out her latest confection— the bride had okayed the cake, so the rest of it was free to be eaten now—and cut it into massive slices, along with diet sodas, announcing it was party time.

Natalie's new husband, Cooper, brought in the twins, Rose and Lily, to meet Molly and share in the impromptu party. The twins, outdoor kids and definitely not dolly-and-tea party kids either, were making friendly overtures. Molly responded with clear reluctance until Natalie brought out the cake and Rose didn't rush for her slice.

"Don't you want any?" Molly asked Rose.

"I've got diabetes," Rose replied with a shrug as she watched her sister cramming cake down her throat. "I can't eat anything with that much fat or sugar."

Molly's hand froze, halfway to her mouth with a handful of cake. "That sucks."

Rose shrugged again. "Mom has it, too. She makes us stuff Lily and Cooper aren't allowed to eat, just to make things fair."

"Don't you get mad? Or sneak stuff when your mom isn't looking?"

Rose made a wry face. "No way. I was in hospital before. I couldn't stop sleeping, and when they gave me the stuff to wake me up, I felt sick and my head hurt for ages."

"She nearly died," Lily mumbled through a mouthful of cake. "Mom really freaked. Cooper saved her." She grinned over at her new stepfather. "It's pretty cool having a dad who can save you when you need it. And I got lots of pizza and ice cream after we visited Rose."

"Whoa." Molly sounded awed, as if almost dying had been an adventure.

She fired question after question about it, but became frustrated after a few minutes by Rose's vague "dunno" answers to questions about how it had felt to be almost dead.

She abandoned the subject after sliding a contemptuous look Julie's way, sharing her exasperation. Then she joined Lily in cake shoveling.

The other Belles were hiding grins or smothering laughs—but Julie felt a niggling sense of unease. She glanced at Matt, in conversation with Callie's husband, Jared, who'd just arrived. Noticing the way his eyes travelled constantly to Molly, and the tiny frown between his brows, she resolved to talk to him about it when they were alone.

It occurred to her that, for the first time in months, she didn't want to avoid being with him. The anger and resentment was still simmering beneath her worry, but it was obvious Matt was clueless about his own daughter—and that, though he needed her help, Molly needed her more.

If Matt could forgive her for losing Molly in the first place.

The party broke up half an hour later. Rose and Natalie were both on strict diet and insulin regimes, not to mention that it was close to bed-time.

Matt thanked everyone for their help in finding Molly. He nudged his daughter when she responded with an eye roll, and shoved her MP3 player earpieces in. Everyone could hear the angry-girl music playing, she had it on so loud.

"Thanks," she said on a heavy sigh, and waved at the twins, nodding and saying, "yeah, all right, cool," when they invited her to play. "You don't play with dolls or anything, do you?" Her disgust was blatant.

"Molly."

Another eye roll. "Dolls are for sissies and little kids, Dad," she explained with such exaggerated patience, and such a "duh"-sounding "Dad," even the twins laughed.

Julie shot a glance at Matt, who was also doing his best not to stare at his daughter. The blank look in his eyes told her the shock was unfeigned.

This was the first time Molly had ever called him Dad. Even said in that insulting way, and within two hours of running away, she'd called him Dad? Again Julie's mind spun. This child had unexpected depths.

Like father, like daughter.

They parted with half promises on Molly's part to play in the *cool* tree house Cooper had just finished building for the twins last week. She even waved goodbye as Matt gently pushed her through the door.

Julie ran down the stairs as Matt closed the passenger's door, with a look of weary frustration that told her Molly had just locked him out again. "Matt."

He looked up, blowing out a sigh, but smiled. "Sorry. Did you need something?"

"No, but it looks like you could use some help settling her in," she said softly. "Want me to come over?"

The relief that washed over his face was almost ridiculous, but was so heart-warming she almost forgot she was furious with him. "Please. Would you?"

Despite her best intentions, Julie felt her face break out into a smile. "I'll be a few minutes behind you."

He tipped her face up and kissed her, slow, sweet and filled with gratitude. "You don't know what it means to me, given what we've both put you through today—especially me. Don't think

I don't know what I've done to you. I want you to know I appreciate your strength and grace, considering you must want to hit me."

The words were exactly what a McLachlan would say—but the kiss was the first they'd shared in weeks. Her tummy was doing flip-flops, big-time, her heart was racing and she felt as if he'd just handed her the moon and stars. "Be right there." Her voice was breathy, filled with the arousal he could inspire in her with the simplest touch. She turned quickly, before he could see it. "I'll see you there."

"Julie."

She turned back, dread pooling inside her, terrified of what he was about to say. Dizzy with all the changes he could inspire in her body and emotions in one minute.

But his smile was filled with gratitude. "You're a Trojan. Thanks for coming—for knowing what to say and do with her." He shrugged. "Today's debacle proves how little I know her, or I'd have realised she was scared and wanting to run away." He turned away; the words were mumbled, almost inaudible. "I feel so stupid."

Feeling something akin to fear—absurd, considering this man was her lover and her fiancé—she reached out and touched his arm. "If I can help…"

He lifted his hand and twined his fingers around hers, his eyes deep crystal blue. "You already have. She likes you. Right now that's more than I can say for me."

"I'm the one who lost her," she replied, disgusted with herself. "I should have realised she'd try—"

Beep!

They both started at once; Julie gasped and jumped. The gleeful, wanting-to-be-bored-but-not-quite-pulling-it-off face emerged from behind the wheel. "It's cold in here. We going or what?"

Matt lifted a brow and made a rueful face. "I'll see you at home."

Julie grinned, nodded and ran back inside The Wedding Belles for her bag and keys, trying to bury the crazy mass of emotions churning inside her—at least for now.

"It sucks here. Look at the room—it's *pink*. I hate eating toast and beans cuz Matt orders a sucky dinner. I hate it here. I wanna go home. Why didn't Mom leave me with Grandma?"

Standing in the hallway outside the room he'd had specially prepared for Molly, Matt winced. He should have known a pink room would be a big mistake. He'd ordered a bad dinner, and all the food he'd bought for her she'd disliked, calling it little-kid food. That left her to eat beans on toast.

Clearly Molly had hated all the kinds of food he'd given her on his trips to Florida.

How little he knew his own daughter.

He drew closer, peeking in. Molly sat at her dressing table, in front of the mirror, and Julie stood behind, brushing his daughter's hair.

"You've never spent time here with your dad before?" Julie asked softly, pulling the brush through, braiding it for the night. Only two minutes ago Molly had told Julie that Kirsten always braided her hair at night, so it waved in the morning. Molly loved the routine and the look.

Right, and thanks for telling me, Kirsten.

Kirsten's list of Molly's likes and dislikes hadn't included Chinese takeout, either. Go figure, a kid who actually *liked* vegetables and home cooking…and she had a biological father who couldn't boil eggs without burning them.

Apparently Dan the Man cooked the *best* lasagne with vegetables in it, and his Sunday roasts were legendary in the family.

"No, cuz it sucks here," Molly snapped. "This place is cold all the time, like a church or something. Like you always gotta whisper."

"I see." Julie's voice was grave, but Matt

could hear the quiver of laughter beneath. "I kinda thought it sucked here at first, too. In Boston, I mean, not the house, though I agree— I've never felt as if I can put my feet up here or dance around the house or yell if I want."

Matt frowned, thinking of Julie's first reaction to his home, of how long it had taken her to stay here overnight, to come here to make love instead of her cosy apartment.

His mom had moved out to her own place in upstate New York within weeks of his dad's sudden death, a heart attack at the office. *I can't stay here anymore, Matt. I need somewhere I can feel happy.*

It seemed none of the most important people in his life liked the house he'd lived in all his life.

"You don't like it here, either?" Molly twisted around, and the braid came out of Julie's hand, unraveling.

"I didn't at first." Without rebuke, Julie turned Molly's head back and re-braided what had come undone. "Boston's nothing like Sydney, where I grew up. Sydney's warm most of the time, and it's a young city. It hasn't got all these old buildings, which are beautiful. But it's not home. And Sydney is more—I don't know—*relaxed* might be it. The people in

Australia are pretty laid-back. And my family's there, too. I miss them a lot."

"Yeah. My mom and grandma and uncle and stuff are all in Florida." A little quaver came and went in Molly's voice. "How long have you lived here?"

"Nearly four years." Julie brushed through the lower half of Molly's hair. "And you know what?" she said so softly, Matt had to strain to hear it. "Even though Sydney will always be home to me, I'd really miss it if I left Boston."

"Oh." Matt could almost see the wheels turning in Molly's head. "How come?"

"It's grown on me, I guess. The city really is pretty. I like the sense of history here, too. I've got a great job, wonderful friends—and your dad's here." A little quiver, similar to Molly's, came and went in Julie's voice.

And this time Matt didn't have to interpret it. She had more to say to him.

The pounding in his head upgraded from moderate to severe. He'd better go take something for it, because the day from hell hadn't yet finished.

"So?" But instead of belligerence, there was genuine curiosity in Molly's tone.

"So, your dad and I are engaged. Remember?" A pause as Molly inspected the diamond solitaire. "He's part of my life now."

"Yeah, he's getting married, too." It wasn't a question, but flatly spoken. "In, like, a couple of *weeks*."

"Your dad should have told you before you arrived today." That wasn't a question, either. "No wonder you were so upset when we met."

"What kind of dad is he? Doesn't he want me to come to his wedding?"

To Julie's credit, she said only, "Your dad's been under a lot of strain lately. I'm sure he was going to invite you, Molly."

"He treats me like a little kid." Molly's voice was loud with disgust. "I was Mom's maid of honour, and *he* doesn't even ask me to come to his wedding. He doesn't tell me anything, and then he brings me here and gives me kid's cereal and milk and microwave burgers? Yuck!"

He'd have to make them industrial-grade painkillers. He'd never heard so many of his faults in one day—and he couldn't refute a single one. The truth of the old bromide of eavesdroppers hearing no good of themselves had been true and then some. He turned and walked down the hall to the stairs.

One thing he was certain about: he was about to have his faults served to him on a platter by the fiancée who probably wouldn't be his fiancée very much longer, given the hell today had been.

Just about on par with the mess of the past few months.

CHAPTER FIVE

"MOLLY'S asleep," Julie said from the doorway of Matt's study. He was at his desk, looking bleak, and no wonder. What a day.

"Thanks," he said, breaking into her thoughts with that dark, singer's voice. "I doubt she'd have slept for me."

Then he smiled at her, and she caught her breath, her stomach flipped and her heart pounded. All the stupid clichéed reactions she'd thought were hooey until the day she'd fallen at a man's feet and looked up at him, laughing at her clumsiness, willing to share the joke.

Then his eyes had met hers, and when he'd smiled she'd forgotten what day it was, where she was and what she'd been doing; she'd forgotten everything but Matt.

Even now, without trying, he'd turned her body into heated honey, ready for him.

She'd avoided him all these weeks because

she still could barely control her reaction to him, even when she wasn't sure if he loved her—when she didn't know if he'd ever loved her. When she no longer knew whether she wanted to stay or bolt.

But one thing she did know: wanting him this way could so easily make her his door-mat. She'd been that once, with Peter Blake, and he'd just been using her to get to Veronica in the end.

That kind of dependence, that humiliation, would never happen again while she was breathing. She couldn't give up the person she was, the woman she wanted to become...not even for Matt.

So Julie forced herself out of slumberous passion, and even dredged up a smile. "She's used to the female touch, and she misses her mother."

"Don't soften it. She'd have gone to sleep for Dan the Man." Matt's eyes grew icy with indefinable emotion as he rubbed his forehead, but this time he didn't lock her out. "The sad truth is that I don't know my own child."

Despite her private agreement, she squelched a desire to say, "Look in the mirror," and said instead, "She lives two thousand miles from you. That was Kirsten's choice."

"Thanks for being nice, but I don't deserve

your support—or for you to sugar-coat the truth. I was outside Molly's room, waiting to say good night, and heard you talking." He shrugged. "Given what I heard, it's no wonder Kirsten left to be with her family in Florida. Molly doesn't like it here, doesn't like the city or my house—and she doesn't like *me* unless I'm giving her presents and fun."

She stared at him, but she was looking at herself in the mirror of his eyes. Matt had been going through so much for so long, while McLachlan's almost collapsed and his father had just died, and while she'd supported and loved him through it all, lately all she'd thought of was her own homesickness, how his abstraction affected her—in other words, it was all about what *she* needed from him.

Perhaps she'd just discovered the reason why Matt found her hard to confide in. Maybe some of their problems were of her creation.

"She loves you, Matt—she's just lost now," she told him earnestly. "Her world has changed with Kirsten's marriage, though she obviously loves Dan. She was brought here without her permission, dumped with a father who's stressed out about his own life and can't give her the routine and family life she loves, and she's reacting to all of that as only a kid can—by acting out."

"Knowing the truth doesn't make it easier to deal with if you don't have the weapons for the fight." His eyes were like a still lake at evening: deep, almost sombre. "You don't like it here, either."

She felt herself blush. He'd obviously overheard that part of the conversation, too. The words were just above a whisper. "I shouldn't have said anything to Molly before I'd spoken to you."

He shrugged. "It made her more comfortable, knowing she wasn't alone. Whatever works, right?" He glanced up with a glimmering smile.

She felt a grin twitching her mouth. How well he knew her. "Right."

"Were you going to move in here, still hating the house?" he asked quietly.

"I don't hate it." She shrugged, feeling stupid again. "It's just...formal. It warns you against singing, dancing, making a mess, tripping over a rug, or doing anything fun that might offend it." She hesitated, then said it. Only total honesty could help them find their way through this maze of resentment and anger they were in. "It reminds me of your father, and how much he disliked me."

"My father ordered most of this stuff. And you're right, this house is formal and cold—all the things you're not." But he was smiling again. "Would it help if I said, go for it? Do what you like to make it more of a place you'd be happy in?"

Sudden confusion filled her, wanting and gladness and fear, and the urge to hit him for making her head spin so much today. Agreeing to redecorate the house would mean she was going to marry him in six short weeks. How could she say that until she was certain of how they both felt?

Would he give her a free run in his house if he wanted to end the engagement? But then, a perfect gentleman never ended an engagement. He'd gently steer her toward ending it. But he wasn't doing that, either.

So what *was* he doing?

If he's confusing me, it's not his fault—at least not today. It's been an emotional wringer for us both.

It certainly wasn't his fault that she ached and pulsed with desire just looking at him, and that it was growing worse by the moment.

"How about Molly and I redecorate her room, to start?" she offered, trying to get a grip on her body's needs. "Since I gather you arranged with The Belles to give me time off. I can take her shopping for things she likes."

"I won't apologise for that, Julie," he said quietly. "I tried for weeks to talk to you. You gave me no other choice."

She held up a hand. Right now she didn't want to fight. "I know." With an effort she grinned. "Back to Molly. I think a few beach posters and some of her favourite singers' pictures might help cover most of the pink." She grinned. "That is, if I could risk offending the hallowed McLachlan walls by sticking up girl-rockers with pins and Blue-Tack."

He stared for a moment before he visibly relaxed and grinned back. "The walls might fall down in shock," he said gravely, "or my father and grandfather might spin in their graves—but I meant what I said. I'll keep up my end of the bargain." He infused his voice with mock long-suffering. "I'll even come along for the choosing of the colour schemes and posters. I need to know my daughter," he said with a shrug. "That is, if I'm welcome." Though his voice was dark, there was a tentativeness beneath that touched her.

He wanted to come. He wanted to get close to Molly.

"Of course you're welcome to come—but can you afford the time off work?"

"I'll make time. This is my daughter."

An aching feeling hurt her chest. The pretty words didn't sound anything but truthful, when he was talking about Molly. He'd make time for Molly. He wouldn't fob her off with excuses about work. "Of course," she murmured, and turned away.

"Julie—" She heard him sigh and mutter something. "I know I screwed up big-time by putting work first for so long. This time I won't leave everything to you, okay? I want to help you. I have to get to know Molly. And besides—" his eyes twinkled, like glittering ice on a pond "—I'm overdue some time off. I don't think the boss will argue."

Despite the pain, Julie chuckled before she could catch it. How he could make her laugh and want to cry all at once was a mystery she couldn't figure out—but that was Matt. He could make her *feel*—

That dark, summer voice sounded right behind her. "It's so good to hear you laugh again."

She stiffened with the feel of his breath on her skin, warm, intimate—arousing. "Don't," she whispered.

"Don't what, Jules?" he asked, very softly. Air from inside his lungs washed over her, moved her hair. "Don't come near you—or don't want you? You can ask for the first, but the second is impossible. While I'm alive, while I'm breathing, I'll hunger to touch you, to be part of you."

She shivered. Her knees wobbled, she was so weak with wanting…

"You don't need to make me feel wanted to help you with Molly." She was shocked by the coolness in her voice, when she was so *hot* inside. "I get it, Matt. You said you needed me. I now know why. So let's get on with it." She headed for the door. "Come to the kitchen, and I'll give you your first dad lesson in how to impress Molly."

"Damn it, Julie," he growled right near her ear, sending hot shivers right down her spine. "I'll go along with most things you want, but I won't lie to you. I want you like hell. Just like I have from the moment I saw you. That will never change, whether I say it or not."

"Stop it," she whispered. She shook her head, and forced herself to say, "If you want me to help you with Molly, I'm here. You want to be a good father, I'll help you. You don't need to…" She couldn't say more. "The things you say…" She waved a hand in a helpless gesture. "I can't deal with it all at once, Matt. You fix things with Molly. She has to be top priority, right?"

"Damn it, Jules." His sigh was pure frustration. "You've got my head in a noose. You know I can't afford to say no."

She bit her lip but nodded and turned away before he could see her eyes were shimmering with tears. "I can only help you with Molly if things between us are—" she scrambled for the right thing to say "—not heavy." She shrugged. "Maybe, if we learn to be friends, things will be better for us."

Right, and she believed it, didn't she? She could be friends with Matt. She could look at him, be with him night and day without aching to touch him, but she needed all her strength just to cope with the family dynamics here.

"Friends. Right." He gave a humourless laugh. "I have no choice, do I?" After a moment he said, "You said something about a lesson to impress Molly. Right now I need all the help I can get." He put his hand on her shoulder, light and impersonal. "I'll take what I can get, and I'll thank you."

If she spoke now, she'd have to show how much his touch was affecting her. She'd become totally breathless and her body was screaming, *such a long time since we made love...*

Screaming, *Touch him, just touch him...*

She pulled away from his hand and all but ran

to the kitchen. "First lesson will be making a good hot chocolate," she croaked, hearing the sensual longing in her voice and cursing it. Wanting him so much it was pain.

He was right behind her again. She could feel his body, hot and wanting, speaking the words his mouth could not.

Moving away from him so fast she nearly tripped, she balanced herself on the counter for a few moments before she opened the cupboards. "You still have chocolate, right? You had a big canister here the last time—" The blush scorched her cheeks. *The last time I stayed over.* "I made some for us." *In bed.* Without meaning to, she moaned.

"Yes."

Julie closed her eyes at the rough sensuality he could infuse into a single word. He was thinking what she was thinking….

She turned to face him, and the hard desire in his eyes made her shiver with need. "This isn't working. Molly's asleep. Maybe I should go."

"No. We can do this. We can try to be friends—for Molly's sake." The fire in his eyes disappeared in an instant, doused by hard anxiety. "I hate being near you without touching you—right now it's killing me—but

God help me, she's only seven. If I wake up to find she's disappeared again, and in danger…" He shuddered. "I need you to teach me how to do the things she likes, to play, to make food she'll eat. I don't want to lose my daughter." A short pause, then he said in a voice rough with pain, "If you ever meant it when you said you loved me, Julie, don't go."

This time she shivered right down to her toes, but not in sensuality. He'd made a heartfelt plea. *He needed her,* if it was only to help him connect to his daughter.

Was it a start?

If you ever meant it when you said you loved me…

A small frisson of shock ran through her. Did that mean she wasn't the only one feeling lost, wondering where the love had gone…if she'd ever been loved?

They'd fallen so hard and fast in love before they'd gotten to basics—and she'd led the chorus. She'd known he was quiet, almost reclusive. She hadn't let it matter. Just being near him was all she'd wanted. Having Matt's love was the most beautiful thing she'd ever known.

She'd told him all she wanted was him, just as he was. Was it his fault if he'd taken her at her word? If she didn't know him now, wasn't part of it her own fault? Didn't she owe it to him—to herself—to try?

"All right, I'll stay tonight," she whispered. "But I need space, Matt. So much is going on. I don't know how I feel about everything you've told me, today and after the party. I need time to work things out."

"I expected that." He was so close to her, his return whisper touched her hair; his breath touched her skin, warm and sensual. "Your being here is more than I deserve, Julie. I won't pressure you. I won't touch you, so long as you're here. Just stay here until she goes home."

She turned to him, and the aching grew stronger. She could never look at him without beautiful pain deep inside her body, wanting, *wanting*. "Stay?"

"Please." His gaze held suffering and bewilderment and a terrible, gnawing fear, an abandonment of the McLachlan pride, the perfect, polite reserve. His eyes held the crystal heart of beauty she could never resist. "If you teach me how to make Molly happy, so I won't have to worry that I'll wake up to find her on the next train back to Florida—or, God help me, hitching a ride with a pervert—I won't pressure you for anything else. Just give me these two weeks, and if at the end of that time you still don't love or want me, we'll call it off."

Shock ran through her again, even though she'd been half expecting him to say something like that for weeks. But what did it mean for them? What did he want from her, apart from help with Molly? "Matt, I…"

Without warning, his face hardened. "Don't lie to me, Julie. Not now. I've given you honesty today, even when it hurt. Don't lessen it with pretence."

"I won't." Slowly she shook her head. "I just don't know how I feel about us right now." Her throat thickened, but she made herself say it. "I won't spend my life with a man who won't share his life with me." She looked up at him, hungering and aching and wishing she were in his arms, and a thousand miles away. "I won't stay with you this way, Matt. I won't spend the rest of my life wondering if I've made a mistake, wondering if we ever really loved each other, or if it was just infatuation and loneliness on my part, and…and duty and kindness on yours." The effort to speak was getting harder by the moment, but he deserved to know. "Great sex and rewarding me for helping you through the bad times isn't a good enough basis for a lifetime."

"I don't believe you." He turned away, mouth

tight. "So long as you stay here and help me with Molly, I'll give you time before I answer that. Our personal life can't be my first priority right now, in any case." He turned and pressed a tight-balled fist on the wall, the knuckles white. "Molly's attitude tends to make me forget she's still so little. She's so much like me, I tend to fight back and think later." The admission seemed to be from a man on the edge of a precipice that scared the hell out of him. "She needs you more than she needs me. Just stay until Kirsten comes back for her."

If it was emotional blackmail, it was also stark need…and Julie felt her tiny store of resistance melt in a heated puddle at his feet. "I'll stay," she whispered. "I'll stay as long as…as long as *Molly* needs me," she added quickly, remembering his words earlier. *If you ever meant it when you said you loved me…* "Now, lesson one—making kid-lovable hot chocolate." She jumped in before he could respond to her palpable uncertainty, the unspoken question. "Then you can go to the all-night store and buy apple-cinnamon oatmeal and some fresh milk, and you can dazzle Molly in the morning with the breakfast she loves."

"I need—" He gave a strangled sigh. "Damn it, I'll keep my word. No point since you don't believe anything I say, anyway." He looked anywhere but at her as he opened the right cupboard for the chocolate. "I'll go to the store now, and I can do two lessons at once. I'll be right back."

Julie sighed as he left the room faster than he used to when they were lovers. *I need you, Julie.* She knew he'd been about to say it—but that was for Molly's sake. Everyone else in Matt's life, apart from his mother, were workaholic overachievers. He had no one else to help him with Molly.

So they were both still lost in the dark maze. She felt unloved, and she doubted he knew what he felt...apart from his obvious love for his daughter.

And that just wasn't good enough to base a lifetime on.

"Why doesn't my hot chocolate taste as good as yours?"

It was over an hour later. Julie didn't have to try to work out how he felt; Matt sounded completely frustrated. She bit the inside of her lip to stop from smiling. "Cooking is an art, Matt. It's as complicated as learning a spreadsheet or payroll. It takes time—and respect."

He lifted a brow, and then a grin formed. He

held up a hand in capitulation. "Okay, then, what did I do wrong? It's hot, it's all fluffy—"

"You thought and cooked as an adult. You scorched the milk," she said patiently. "Boiled milk does fluff up, it looks good and it tastes good with cappuccino, but it doesn't make a kid-friendly hot chocolate—and kids expect to drink their hot chocolate the moment it's put before them. So you only serve it warm for a seven-year-old."

"Ah." His eyes lit with comprehension. "Take two. Just as well I bought three cartons of milk."

Julie allowed the smile this time. "And it's good you bought two packets of oatmeal, as well, since we haven't even started on the hard stuff yet."

He blew out an exaggerated sigh, emptied the pot, rinsed it and scrubbed off the scorched milk before starting over.

Again her heart melted, watching him trying and failing for his daughter's sake, and trying over again. His brow was all knitted with concentration over the important task of what temperature to take the milk off the heat, as he stirred the oatmeal and turned it down to low with all the air of a prophet; making something soften inside her.

Whoa. Hold it there, sister. Everything he's done today only proved his love for Molly.

Having met Matt's father a grand total of four times before his heart attack, she knew how the exquisite McLachlan manners could hide a range of emotions she couldn't see. Matt's father said everything beautifully, but he'd thought her a temporary thing, a quick affair yet unworthy of sharing a lifetime with his son. She'd seen that from the first, even if Matt hadn't.

Though, Matt's here with his illegitimate daughter, refusing to hide her or leave her behind. It's Matt I'd be spending my life with. His father's gone.

But still—

"But what? What did I do? Is it too hot again, or scorched? I was hoping I'd finally made it right this time?"

With a start she came back to the present. She was sipping Matt's fourth attempt at hot chocolate now—more like *Eau de chocolat,* really, since he'd switched to his designer flavoured and scented chocolates, this one Chocolat Noisette, to save on Molly's sachets. "No, it's just right." With another effort—dear God, the man made her ache so badly with wanting she could barely think—she smiled. "Molly will love it."

"And the oatmeal?" he asked in a gruff tone that barely hid his anxiety. "You haven't touched it."

With a Herculean effort, she managed not to screw up her face. Molly's favourite breakfast of oatmeal wasn't Julie's favoured food at any time, and cinnamon was a particular pet hate—and this was his third effort she'd had to taste-test. She smiled again, lifted a spoonful to her mouth and ate half, putting the spoon back into the bowl. "Perfect," she mumbled behind her hand, through the hot mouthful. And it was definitely his best effort.

"She says bravely, eating half a spoonful when I know how much you dislike oatmeal. Thanks, Julie. You've been a lifesaver tonight." He leaned into her, and she breathed in the fresh, masculine essence of him with a deep sigh of feminine appreciation.

But the brushing of his lips across her cheek—that gorgeous, almost-pouting mouth just touching the side of hers—made raging thirst for *Eau de Matt* rip through her, unstoppable, uncontrollable.

Her hands were on his skin before she could curl her fingers over.

"Thank me properly, and I'll teach you how to make dinner tomorrow, with a guarantee Molly will love it," she whispered thickly, leaning into him. Winding her hands into his hair...*ah*, touching him again. It was good, so good...

"More blackmail, Jules?" he mumbled against her mouth as he wrapped his arms around her waist, dragging her close at the speed of light. There was a smile in his voice.

"Uh-huh," she mumbled back, and kissed him once, twice. "Ransom demanded for every good deed."

"We're beyond saving, you know that," he mumbled between hot, clinging kisses. "We can never be just friends when it's like this for us all the time."

Right now she didn't care. "Mmmm..." She opened her mouth and took the kiss higher, deeper. Moving against him, she felt the male arousal—*Matt*—with a long sighing moan into his mouth.

The next thing she knew they were on the antique sofa in the den, twined around each other, his hand shaped around her breast, and she was arching into him, moaning and whimpering with need. Her leg hooked around his hip, keeping him a willing prisoner. How they'd gotten there she neither knew nor cared. *Oh*, he was kissing down her throat, bringing every single part of her body to life with his thumb against the peak of her breast, and her hands were happy at last, under his shirt and sweater to feel silky-hot skin and rough hair.

Take me to bed, she almost whispered.

Then she froze as panic washed through her. If she made love with him now, she'd be in so deep she'd never be able to leave him. She'd barely survived the past eight weeks, aching for him day and night.

But she couldn't be his satellite, his support and cheering squad, her needs submerged while he still didn't share with her…

"Stop," she whispered.

His hands and mouth stilled. She felt the long breath in and out, before he bent and kissed the tips of her breasts through her clothes, with lingering sweetness and desire.

A tiny cry tore from her throat.

Then he got to his feet and began rearranging his clothes. "Thank you, for Molly's sake if not for mine," was all he said, his voice hoarse.

Julie closed her eyes, felt the pain of denial tearing through her body. "That wasn't why I stopped it," she said quietly.

"I know," he said, just as quiet, hiding the pain and need and denial.

She saw the mirror of her need in his eyes—and the weary acceptance that, much as he wanted to, they couldn't make love. With a sigh of painful frustration, she pushed at him. "I'll wash up."

He got to his feet, and helped her up. "I'll help."

She shook her head. "No, go check on Molly."

"Jules?"

Hearing the darkness of uncertainty in his voice, she gulped, hating herself. Hating that she'd made him so insecure; hating herself for her lack of self-control. Sex wasn't going to fix their problems; it would just give him hope that she'd accept him as he was. There were too many secrets, and too much pain.

She was only here now because Matt loved his daughter; he'd kidnapped her only because he'd needed her help. He hadn't bothered trying anything so dramatically romantic for her sake alone.

Yes, keep reminding yourself of that, she thought grimly.

She met his questioning gaze. "I said I wouldn't lie to you. I want you like crazy, so please go away. Every second you're near me makes it worse. I'm here for Molly, not to make love with you. It's not enough."

The smile that had begun with her second sentence died with the third. "Damn it, Julie, I'm trying, can't you see that? I'm telling you things close to my heart!"

"For Molly's sake," she retorted, low. "It's all for Molly's sake. Which proves only one thing—that you love your daughter. I'm glad of that, but—"

"It's not enough," he snarled, surprising her with the depth of his anger. "I've been the one trying to communicate the past eight weeks!"

"Only because Kirsten called you and you were stuck in a hole. You needed me to help you with Molly. You never told me a single thing before then—and anything else came from the reporter. I...I don't even know if you'd have told me about that, even now..." She hiccupped again and swallowed savagely. She would *not* cry, like a sniveling child!

"And you don't believe a word I say. So what can I do, produce documentary evidence? I don't have it. All I can say is I've never lied to you, Julie—about anything."

She just looked at him; they both knew she didn't have to say it.

He held her gaze, his like an ice storm, cold and hard with truth. "I never lied to you directly, Julie. I left things out, yes—I fobbed you off. But it *was* work. Going to Florida *was* a family issue. And today I've hidden nothing. I've told you the absolute truth."

She sighed and shook her head. "That's nice,

Matt, but I can't comfort myself with that the next time you say something to me and I wonder what you're hiding."

Matt swore and swung away. "I think we've said enough tonight. I won't damage whatever we have left by saying things in anger."

She turned her face from him. If he couldn't see that nothing she'd said had come from anger—that it was all true—then there was no hope at all for them. "Good night," she whispered. "Sleep well."

"Thank you, but I won't sleep well without you," he muttered so low she almost didn't hear him. "But at least tonight has taught me one thing."

That she still wanted him like hell? It was too obvious to deny. "Well?" She waited for the words. He deserved his moment of triumph.

"It's not over, Jules. We're not over." He turned back to face her, his eyes burning into hers. "I might have messed things up, but if you still want me so badly, then you still love me."

The part of her that acknowledged he was right left her feeling as if he'd cut her legs off at the knees. What did he want from her? She was *here*, wasn't she? She was here after all he'd done to deserve nothing from her. But *he* wasn't here, not heart and soul—not for her.

She didn't know, couldn't see his heart, and that hurt most.

She looked at her feet—relieved to see they were still there—and mumbled, "You wanted Kirsten. You have Molly because of that. Did that mean you loved her, or do your standards only apply to me?"

After a few moments he said wearily, "You don't hold back, do you?"

She shuffled her feet. "No. That's why I'm still here when I should have told you to go to hell today. It was all you deserved."

Matt swore again. "Yes, okay—but bloody hell, Jules, don't you get it? I won't let go. I won't lose you. I don't care what I have to do, I'm going to win you back."

The tiny start of shock, of half-forbidden excitement, rippled through her. Had he really said something so raw, so unrehearsed? She opened her mouth to ask what winning her would entail...but then commonsense prevailed, and she stepped back. "It's been a long, hard day, Matt, and I'm too tired to answer. After all the things I've found out about you, the pretty things you say only hurt me and leave me feeling empty."

A short silence. "You don't believe the things I tell you?"

"How can I, since I found out everything you were keeping from me?" She whirled back, angry enough to say the things she'd tried to hold in. "I can't believe them any more than I could believe your father when he told me you needed a change. He smiled at me, he was always a gentleman when we met, but because I wasn't country club or old money, I wasn't good enough for his son, apart from the quick fling he expected. He wanted you to stay with Elise, didn't he?"

After a long moment he said only, "Yes."

"He wanted you to marry her, didn't he?" she murmured, as the truth came to her. "Did he start the rumours you would marry her?"

His voice was tight, hard. "I believe so, yes."

"An old trick, but a good one—and most of the time it works," she said, her throat tight. "He *said* everything beautifully, but didn't mean a word. He steered you in the direction he wanted but didn't *tell* you anything. His secrets remained his own, right to the end. Like father, like son."

Matt's eyes were burning now: fire and blue ice. "I am nothing like my father."

She'd obviously hit a sore point with him, but she couldn't hold back now. He needed to know why she didn't believe in him anymore, before he began to believe that passion was enough—that even love was enough. "Yes, you are. You're a perfect gentleman, but only reveal the parts of yourself that make you look good, never your true and *real* thoughts and feelings. Look at today. You tell me about Molly when she's almost here, and you can't *stand* that she'll make you look like a bad father. But I have brothers and sisters, and have babysat nieces, nephews and neighbourhood kids. Chances are Molly will like me. So you do the romantic kidnap scene, and tell me the truth only when you knew I'd seen through you. Right now, you'll say whatever you think will keep me here, helping you with her."

She knew she'd gone too far by his white face and burning eyes, but some imp inside her made her finish it. "You are your father's son."

Without a word he turned and walked out the door—but by the furious and devastated expression on his face, she knew she'd gone way beyond hurting him—she'd destroyed him.

She opened her mouth to call him back, but closed it before words emerged…because though she hated hurting him, everything she'd said was true. He'd shared some of his life, but only because he'd been forced to tell her. And he hadn't done so until Molly was on her way here.

Matt was right. This wasn't over—not by a long shot, she thought grimly. If he truly wanted her, if he cared beyond the things that made her useful to him, he was going to have to fight for her…and without his plans or his rules.

CHAPTER SIX

MATT didn't have to analyze why he was so furious. All he had to do was remember. *Of course I love you, Anne,* his father had always said during another low-voiced argument. *Why do you always doubt me this way?*

And his father would walk out, leaving his mother to sob in her lonely pillows at night, and Matt to burn with anger. He knew his mother would have called the office hours before, or called the hotel his father was staying at "for the conference," and the same woman answered the phone every time…and she wasn't his father's personal assistant.

He'd sworn at the age of eleven that he'd never be like his father.

It's nothing, Jules, just hassles at work…I love you, Jules.

Suddenly he wanted to throw up. The echoes

of the past came ringing back to taunt him. He'd never cheated on her, never even thought of it, but when Julie began to suspect his worries had been something deeper than just work, when she'd tried to share other parts of his life beyond the romantic and sexual, he'd fluffed her off with excuses that had been exposed for the lies they were when Jemima Whittaker spoke to her about Elise.

Dear God, he *was* like his father in all but one thing—and fidelity alone wasn't enough to keep Julie here. It was a miracle she was still willing to help him with Molly.

She might want him, but she'd come, she'd stayed for Molly's sake—and maybe for the love they'd had in the past.

He'd blown it. He had to stop fooling himself that just because he still loved her she loved him back.

Matt sighed and walked into Molly's room. On a mission to bond with his daughter and his fiancée at one time, he knew he was shooting for the moon, but he had to believe he could do it. No other option.

Matt snuck out of Molly's room moments later, and put her MP3 player earpieces in his own ears. As he listened to the music his daughter liked, he jotted down notes so he could buy her some posters tomorrow without Julie's help; but his mind was on Julie.

She'd promised to stay. He had two weeks to fix this. He already had some clues—enough to make a mental list.

The house was too formal. That was an easy fix: redecorate.

Suddenly he remembered when he was a little boy, thinking there was a bad man or a ghost hiding in the house that wanted to hurt him. Afraid of the bogeyman he was sure lived inside the portrait of his stern-faced great-grandfather, he'd slept in the cupboard until his father had cured him of the habit.

So, make the house more warm and friendly. Done—or soon would be.

Grimly he moved on to problem number two: he hadn't been communicating with either Julie or Molly.

He made a strangled sound. This was like facing his Grandfather-nightmare....

But surely Julie couldn't help but know he needed her now. His inability to cope with Molly was screaming so loud he might as well have blasted it over a loudspeaker. He didn't know what to do with his own child.

Julie had an inborn knack with kids, a relaxed *come here and join my fun* he'd first fallen in love with and Molly had responded to within moments—something he ached for his child to do with him.

The key to winning Molly was to have Julie in his life and learn from her. The key to winning Julie was showing her how much he needed her. Not *telling* her. He had to *show* her how he felt, all of it—the good, the bad and the humiliating. He'd talk to her, share his worries and hopes and dreams with her.

He could do that. All he had to do was change the habits of a lifetime, to find a way to change a part of himself that was so intrinsic he didn't even think about it.

He laid his head against the wall, resisting the urge to whack it.

It was about time for that miracle he'd been praying for.

"Eeew. This is disgusting."

Standing behind the kitchen door the next morning, still in her PJs, Julie leaned against the wall, waiting to see if she should go in to help or let him try again. Poor Matt, failing with such a simple thing as Molly's breakfast—

"I know," Matt said to his daughter, but though he sounded apologetic, he didn't sound crushed. "Julie showed me how to make oatmeal for you, but I've always been a terrible cook. Sorry, Molly."

"That's okay. So's Mom, really," Molly confided cheerfully. "We call Dad Dan the Man cuz he's the one who cooks and cleans and looks after us."

"Really? I don't remember that about your mom."

"That's cuz you two weren't together very long. Mom doesn't know much about you, either." Julie heard a scraping sound. "Oatmeal's easy. Let's do it again. Dad says the trick is to never stop stirring it, and add some brown sugar and cinnamon, even with the packet mix. He says they never put in enough for kids."

"Okay, but how much of each do we need?"

Julie heard the evenness in Matt's voice, not reacting to Molly's calling Dan 'Dad.' Probably he recognised, as Julie did, that right now Molly wasn't using it to hurt him. Matt was her father; Dan was 'Dad.' One of those child-facts in life kids take on without question and adults find so hard to accept.

How it must hurt Matt, the more so for the fact that Molly wasn't doing it to provoke him.

"I dunno," Molly answered Matt after a few seconds, "but Dad always gets a clean spoon and tastes it before he gives it to me, and adds more if it's not good."

"We can do that. How about we try a teaspoon at a time, and you tell me when it tastes good?"

Molly laughed. "Why don't I just eat it straight from the pot?"

Matt laughed with her. "Sounds great to me." He went on, using the very words she'd used on him a year ago. "It'll save on washing up— but we won't tell Julie about it, okay? I might get in trouble for letting you do it. Big girls tend to get fussy about eating from the right bowl or plate, and eating at the table."

Julie covered her mouth with her hand to stop the bark of laughter from emerging. She wondered if he'd ever *not* eaten at the table with a full contingency of crockery and cutlery before she'd taught him the joys of eating in front of the fire, the TV—and off each other's skin….

She groaned to herself just thinking about it.

"Yeah, tell me about it," Molly replied in total sympathy. "Mom's always saying to get my elbows off the table and stuff. I mean, who *cares* where your elbows are, anyway?"

"Moms do. Good thing I'm just a dad, huh?"

More shared laughter, Matt's deep, bell-like chuckle blending beautifully with Molly's childish, silver-gold giggle.

Julie smiled and snuck back down the hall, leaving father and daughter to their bonding time, shaking her head in wonder. Matt sure was a fast learner….

Which means he won't need me for very much longer. A few more days, and it'll be over.

Trying to tell herself it was for the best, she walked back upstairs for her shower.

"I'm sorry for the short notice, Belle, but Matt's not used to kids, even his own. Her room needs redecorating, he can't cook for her, and he doesn't know what to do to make her happy, so she doesn't take off again. He needs me here until he and Molly settle into a routine together. And with my family arriving soon, I need to get things ready. Hopefully I should only need a few days—"

"That's just fine, darlin'," Belle answered, and Julie could hear the smile in her voice. "I told you yesterday, take two weeks off. You're overdue the time, apart from your honeymoon leave. Most brides need a few weeks before the wedding to organise things. Since the wedding's all done, apart from the things Matt—um, it means you and Matt and Molly can enjoy some time together. We'll cope just fine. I'll get Charlie in to answer the phones if

I have to—what's the point of having a man head over heels in love with you if you can't blackmail him now and then?"

A series of stifled chuckles told Julie the call was on speaker, and all the girls were listening in. Julie wanted to laugh herself, imagining old-world, courteous Charlie answering the phone at a wedding business, discussing flowers and the advantages of salmon foie grâs appetisers over pâté and caviar with anxious brides and their mothers.

"There'll be a stampede of women making bookings if Charlie's there for long. I'd better watch out, I might lose my job."

"Never, darlin'. We need you," Belle said softly. "We can do without you for a few weeks, but you're pretty near indispensable, don't you know that? We all love you, Julie. You have the knack of makin' most everyone adore you in moments—somethin' I'm certain your man knows well, which is why he kidnapped you yesterday."

"Thank you, Belle," she said, resigned to the fact that Belle and the girls were misconstruing her reasons for wanting time off. Her friends were the worst kind of romantics: cynics who'd each been converted to love by finding their own Mr. Right. Though she'd said nothing, she guessed it had been obvious that she and Matt were having problems, and the Belles wanted to help. Time alone with Matt was bound to bring the romance back.

She only wished it were that simple.

"Did you know about Molly, Julie?" Regina, the closest friend she had at the Belles, asked softly.

Julie bit her lip. That was Regina; she could cut to the heart of her problem with a gentle slash. "No," she said quietly.

Absolute silence met the word. She knew what they were all thinking. *What on earth is she still doing with that man?*

She wondered that herself. Wondered how he still made her feel so much…

"I'm sorry, Jules," Audra finally said, sadness in her voice.

"It's okay." She said goodbye before the awkward silence stretched out any longer.

As she disconnected the phone, a soft knock sounded at her open door. She looked up to see Matt standing there, with that just-crooked smile that thickened her throat and upped her heart rate. "Are you ready to go? Molly's jumping at the front door. She's so excited about the whole redecorating idea she's forgotten she wants to go home, for now at least. It's pretty warm out there today. No need for a jacket."

It was *pretty warm* in here right now, as well, if her body temperature was any indication, and she was only looking at him.

No, wanting Matt wasn't the problem. The more time she spent with him, the more she wanted him. Right now, instead of posters and paint, all she could think of was that she was sitting on a bed and Matt was right here. If she took him by the hand and closed the door, she could—

She forced a smile and said, "Sure," hoping like crazy that her mind graphics weren't showing on her face. "I was thinking we could take in that fun park after. You know, the one on the way back from the Peabody factory outlets? The more fun we make the stay for Molly, the less she'll think about running home to her grandmother."

"Sounds great," he said, in a low growl. "Do me a favour, though. Control the way you're looking at me now, when Molly's around." He'd crossed the room as he spoke, lifted her hand in his and kissed it, soft and lingering. "The physical reaction it inspires isn't going to help me think and act like a good dad."

Julie felt her face burning. "Sorry," she mumbled.

He lifted her to her feet. "Don't be," he whispered into her hair. "I've loved the way you look at me right from the time you fell at my feet." And his words didn't feel a bit rehearsed; they pulsed with sexuality that set her whole body on fire.

She moved against him, drinking in his closeness, his touch, barely knowing what she said. "It was that obvious, huh?"

Matt lifted her hair, and kissed her neck. "I never believed it could happen to me, Jules. Not until you looked up at me, put your hand in mine, and gave me your number—before you said hello, before I could even help you to your feet."

"And then I kissed you." Brushing her lips against his cheek.

"As if tomorrow wouldn't come." He kissed the side of her mouth, teasing, arousing.

"I had to. I was so scared you'd forget me and not call." He brushed his mouth over hers, and she was gone. "Matt…" An aching whisper.

It was everything Matt had promised he wouldn't do—*damn* it, she wanted him but didn't know him or like him! He had to keep things light and friendly, give her time to see the man beneath. But when she looked at him like that, as if she'd die if she didn't have him right then, all his good intentions flew out of his head. He molded her to him, shoulder to hip, curving his hand over her butt to keep her locked against his body, loving its rounded softness. Ah, the feel of her taut nipples against his skin through his thin shirt…the way she moaned and moved against him, revelling in his arousal…he groaned and kissed her as if tomorrow *wouldn't* come, as if she'd disappear any moment and this memory would be all he'd have.

And lately, that's exactly how it felt. So while Julie kissed him with all her addictive passion, moaning, mumbling his name between kisses, it didn't feel *safe*. She kissed him as if she didn't want to disappear from his life—

As if she wasn't going to bolt from him the first chance she got. As if she hadn't been torturing him with her uncertainty for the past eight weeks. *Will she still be here tomorrow? Will she let me touch her today, or will she look at me as if she just wished I'd go to hell?*

He couldn't go through it again. He wanted her love, not just to get her into bed again. He wanted her for the rest of his life, not for an hour's loving. Sticking to the plan was his only hope.

Slowly he ended the kiss. "We'd better go."

Julie looked up at him, her summer-gaze blurred with desire. "Huh?"

Man, he loved that look…and he almost got lost again. "Molly's waiting," he said roughly. "The shopping trip? The fun park?"

"Right." She sighed and laid her head on his chest, breathing in and out deeply for almost a minute. Her hands dropped from his body, and for a foolish moment he wished he hadn't spoken. "I'm being a hypocrite. I made it clear you weren't to touch me," she said.

Good resolutions melted. "But I never said you couldn't touch me. We'll make love again soon—and I won't let you out of bed for days." *And I'll never let you out of my life again, not even for a day.*

She shivered, her panting breaths caressing his skin through the open-necked shirt, but he knew the moment was over. "We should go now."

She wouldn't accept his words—worse, she didn't believe him. How the hell was he supposed to win her back if he had to do it without words, and without touching her? *Ay caramba,* this woman was going to kill him one way or another. "I'll go downstairs. Are you ready to go?"

She nodded, her summer-sky eyes distant. "Just need my shoes."

"And I need some self-control." Ruefully, he looked down at what no seven-year-old should see. "I need a cold shower before I go down to Molly…preferably one with ice cubes in it."

Julie bit her lip, but the bubble of sweet mirth escaped. From withdrawal, he'd made her laugh—and it was like she'd given him a shot of something; it brought an instant high.

Maybe he had more weapons than he'd feared. Laughter, Molly, just being himself—let her come to him; let her touch him. And she loved his smile, his eyes. He could use that to his advantage.

As Matt walked downstairs to Molly, he thought again about his plan to bring her back into his life. Seduction without words or touch…when Julie threw out challenges she didn't do things by halves…but maybe Julie was right. They'd fallen in love, become lovers, but while he felt he knew her inside and out, while he'd found the best friend he'd ever known, she'd never gotten to truly know him. If she still wanted that, he could win—if only he could keep talking to her. Friends and lovers worked for a lifetime.

And, given the fire that burned between them with every look, she really had given him the challenge of his life.

CHAPTER SEVEN

WHAT was she doing here?

Here at the furniture factory outlet, standing beside Matt as they watched Molly running from display to shelf with eyes of wonder, she knew that was the trouble.

Why was she still here? She didn't know what would happen next. She had no clue what she wanted. All she knew was, standing here with Matt and watching Molly's delight, she felt happier than she had in a long time.

Despite her fears, her uncertainties, a warm feeling spread across her chest. Within a day, she'd helped a father and daughter come closer together—and, despite her rebelliousness, Molly would need her father in years to come. Though she didn't know it, Molly needed him even now.

She'd done a good thing for Matt and Molly. It was worth the sacrifice of her time, the investment of her emotions.

Is it worth a broken heart?

"Look at this, Julie—isn't it cool?"

Unwilling to answer her own question, she allowed Molly to drag her over to what was obviously a display of a boy's room, black on blue with streaks of silver, with knights and dragons on the bed cover and posters, with a smile she kept hidden.

"Um, Molly, isn't this a—"

Julie elbowed Matt before he could finish the sentence, and he went on, "Um, a very cool room. Which bits do you like best?"

"The dragons," Molly said, without hesitation. "It's like in *The Hobbit,* even the knights in the chain mail stuff."

"You've read *The Hobbit*?" Matt asked, clearly startled.

Molly rolled her eyes. "Duh, Matt. I'm *seven,* and it's got big words. Dad read it to me. It's the coolest book ever. Dad says when I'm twelve we'll start reading *The Lord of the Rings* together. I snuck it out of Dad's room to read it, but it's got even bigger words. Mom took it back. She says I can't watch the movies until I understand the book, because of the scary bits. But I love all the battles and stuff. It's so cool."

So that explained Molly's fascination with Rose's near-death experience—it was an adventure to her. Right…adventure, action, excitement. Julie planned to call her brother, Jason, to see what her sci-fi-loving niece Miranda was reading.

Matt leaned toward her as Molly caressed the long lines of the attacking dragon. "Check—visit a bookstore and ask the clerk what's the latest for sci-fi/fantasy-reading kids. I could read to her at night."

"Good idea," she whispered back. Since she doubted Matt would ever get the hang of braiding hair, it would be good if he could read to Molly.

Matt called over an assistant and ordered the entire bedroom set and arranged for same-day delivery.

Molly's face lit up. She threw herself at Matt, her hug a stranglehold. "You're the *best* biological parent ever!"

Matt laughed and hugged her back. "Hey, Molly, take it easy, I need to breathe." But his face was alight with joy; his eyes held a serenity, a security they hadn't shown for a long time. He winked at Julie over Molly's head, and mouthed, Thank you.

"Thanks for suggesting we come here," he murmured as Molly dashed over to another thing that interested her. "This place is a kid's paradise. Well, a *female* kid's paradise—even an obvious tomboy who wants dragons in her room instead of dollies." He hesitated, then said, "Today's been fantastic. Choosing her own things for the house was an inspired idea. Molly's happy—and it's all thanks to you, Julie." He grinned, looking like a kid himself.

He was happy, because he'd made Molly happy.

Funny, she hadn't thought of Matt as such a family man until the past twenty-four hours. She'd thought of him as her lover, the man she'd loved from first sight—but to her he was first and foremost a businessman, one with a strong streak of conscience and a sense of responsibility to his workers.

But the loving father, the family man? The thought touched Julie, yet left her feeling strange…not quite sad, not quite lost, but as if she was groping to see, to reach an understanding that eluded her. Something was missing, some piece of the puzzle she should know.

Where did she fit into it? Where did Matt want her to fit in—if he did want her at all?

She followed father and daughter to the counter to pay for the bedroom set. If she'd always known Matt as this person, this man who lived for his family's happiness, she might have seen everything differently—including his partnership with Elise.

And if he'd been this man, and if he'd been the one to tell her about his friendship and partnership with Elise, she might just have believed him.

They called this place a *fun* park?

Matt spun around and around in a thing that looked like a teacup, feeling every churning ounce of the juicy steak and salad he'd eaten for lunch. Molly and Julie didn't have a worry in the world, laughing on either side of him as they competed for the wheel, twisting it harder and harder to make it spin faster.

This thing was almost worse than the roller coaster, but not as bad as the thing that looked like a big zipper, when they'd hung upside-down in cages like animals....

Keep eyes open. Focus on something...ah, um, the—no, it was moving...um, his jeans. Yes, he could look down and not think about his heaving stomach and how his eyes felt like they'd pop out any second.

"That was cool! We gotta do that again." Molly swung Julie's hand in hers as Matt staggered down the stairs. "Matt, I'm hungry. Can I have a corn dog?"

"Oh, Go—" He caught himself in time.

"Um...okay." His stomach heaved again, in a painful cramp. "If I give you the money, can you, um, get it yourself?"

Alerted by his tone, Molly peered at him. "Hey, Matt, you're *green!*" She began giggling, and after a moment Julie failed to keep her own laughter down. "What a wuss," Molly chortled. "A little teacup ride and he's gonna barf!"

He wanted to argue that the little teacup ride around and around had followed the up and down of the roller coaster and the upside-down of the zipper ride, and all within half an hour of eating lunch; but unfortunately for his dignity, he was indeed, as she put it, gonna barf. He pushed his wallet at Julie, mumbled, "Excuse me," and bolted.

When he emerged from the men's room, they were waiting for him. Molly was cheerfully grinning at him around the remains of whatever gross confection she'd bought, but Julie laid a gentle hand on his arm. "Are you all right now?"

Feeling totally humiliated, he managed a nod. "Would you mind continuing the rides with Molly? I can mind the toys."

"Yeah, come on, Julie! I wanna go on the Ferris wheel, it's really big. Maybe we'll get stuck at the top!"

Matt groaned as his stomach took fire again.
"Hush, Molly. Matt's not feeling well."
Looking worried, she led him to a bench, and
pushed him into the seat. "Why didn't you tell
me you don't like amusement parks?"

Matt sighed and held his stomach. "It isn't
that. It's that I'm not used to this kind of thing.
I've only been to one once, when I was twelve,
and I went with my school."

Even Molly blinked at that piece of information. "Why not? Didn't your mom and dad like
them? Didn't you ever have a party at a park
with all your friends?"

"I don't think he's up to a discussion right
now, Molly," Julie said, when Matt didn't—
couldn't—answer. "I know you don't like tea,
Matt, but right now it really will help. I doubt
they'd have peppermint or ginger tea, but black
tea will help settle your stomach, too."

Unable to speak further, he nodded. He felt
so damn embarrassed. So much for his plans
for showing Julie the real man. If she judged
him by this...

"Molly, stay here with your dad, okay? I'll be
right back."

Bless Julie for her understanding. Molly
remained silent while Julie was gone, patting
him every few moments, and turning aside

from him when she was shoveling more food in her mouth.

Somebody walked past with a tray of food. Meat, meat and more meat, by the smell of it, plus a ton of mustard and ketchup. Hot dogs, too, and fries.

His stomach revolted. With an inarticulate noise, he bolted back to the men's room.

"I didn't do anything, I promise," Molly was saying earnestly to Julie when he came back. "He just ran off!"

"It's okay, Molly. You didn't do it," he said wearily as he fell into the seat. "I'm just not used to places like this."

Julie handed him the foam cup of tea. "Sip slowly. You'll feel better soon."

He sipped at it, and found she was right: the cramps slowly subsided as he drank more. "Thanks," he said, and even managed a smile.

Molly was hopping from foot to foot. "Can I go to the Laughing Clowns? They've got this great spit-darts set I could win…."

Spit darts and dragons, wild rides and junk food. He marvelled again at the walking, demanding paradox that was his daughter—and at the depth of love he felt for Molly, just as she was.

But she'd run away only yesterday, and the

disappearance haunted him. He looked around and saw the game only twenty feet from them. With a sigh of relief, he said, "Go on." He handed her a ten-dollar bill. "Have a few turns. Win me something, too."

"Cool!" She was gone before she'd spoken, and the word came floating back toward them on a wafting wave of ketchup.

Matt held down the groan, and sipped with slow deliberation at the tea, keeping his eyes on Molly.

"You'll feel better soon," Julie said softly.

He looked around briefly, saw the understanding on her face, and wondered anew. He almost kept it to himself, but she'd told him to talk to her. He had to start somewhere besides Molly. "There's something I don't understand." He switched his gaze back to Molly, noting with relief that she was engrossed in spending his money to win something. So he could begin to make a connection with Julie. "Why is it that when I win, you back off from me, but when I fall on my face, you're there to pick me up?"

She frowned and moved back, the tenderness vanishing.

"No. Don't do it, Julie. I've given you the good, bad and humiliating for twenty-four hours straight." He tipped up her chin, looking into her face, seeing the rich blush covering her cheeks. "Why?" he asked softly, leaning close but not touching.

Her eyes darkened as she looked into his, aching with wanting. "I don't want you to fail, Matt." She wet her mouth, and the pulsing ache grew stronger. "I'm not threatened by your success. But when you're—floundering—you talk to me. You ask for my opinion and my help." The slow blush deepened. "You need me then, Matt. You...you share yourself with me."

He had to acknowledge the truth of that. "I don't know what I'd have done without you this past day, Julie."

She sighed, and her gaze fell. "You wouldn't be in this place but for me."

He could see she was blaming herself for the suggestion of coming here, just as she'd blamed herself when Molly ran away.

He looked around and saw his daughter checking out the Laughing Clowns and handing over her money moments later.

"No, I'd probably be at the police station trying to find where she'd gone again," he admitted with a sigh. "If she was still here, she'd still have a pink room, I wouldn't have half a dozen posters to stick to my hallowed walls, or a 'totally cool' book to read to her tonight. I wouldn't have had a funny disaster with her over breakfast." After a moment he added, "In other words, I still wouldn't have a clue what made my daughter tick, and would only have a nightmare two weeks to look forward to. You changed the dynamics of my relationship with Molly, Julie. It's worth a few trips to the men's room, trust me. I don't regret a thing."

The look of self-blame dissipated, replaced by a half-shy, half-eager glow. She offered him a small, tilting smile that made her look sweet and curious—like a wild bird about to hop on his shoulder. "Today's been…nice. Apart from you feeling sick, of course," she hastened to add. "It's great having Molly here. I've missed— family things like this. Just goofing off."

She was talking to him again, and damn, it felt good. "I wish I'd known how much you needed it." But then, he hadn't known Molly needed it…or even that *he* did. This day, "doing nothing" as his father would contemptuously call it, had revealed so much. He'd learned more about the women in his life during the past six hours in "goofing off" than any amount of study or time in restaurants or in quiet discussion at the country club would have told him.

"Why didn't I know this about you, Jules?" he asked softly, moving an inch closer. Giving her an opening to touch him if she wanted to—and it was radiant, shining from her as she drank in his face, his closeness.

She sighed, and he wondered if he'd blown it again. "Because I didn't think you'd want to do things like this, I guess." She met his gaze with a straight look. "When we met, I walked into your world. Considering that mine, apart from my friends and job, was ten thousand kilometres away, I didn't have much of a world to give you. So I *talked* to you about my life and past, but my present and future was with you." She shrugged. "If I'd known about Molly…"

Yes, it always came back to that, he thought grimly.

As if she heard his thought, she rushed on. "It's probably also because when we spent time alone together, I did most of the talking and you listened." The look she slanted him was wry with self-knowledge. "It wasn't just you who did the wrong thing with us. We both did it backwards, Matt. I guess we're paying the price for that now."

He heard the end in her words. He gripped her hands in his, willing himself to defeat the anger and reach out to her. "Do we have to pay,

Jules? Can't we try to get past this and start over?"

She slanted him an odd, intense look. "Spend time alone and talk? Not touching, not making love?" She laughed, but without mirth. "We didn't even make it past six hours yesterday without almost ripping each other's clothes off, and we had Molly there as a buffer. I thought it was over, and still I couldn't control it."

"We can try," he urged her, unable to deny he was in pain with wanting her. She thought that to connect they had to somehow put aside the magnificent loving? Heaven help him, because he didn't think he could be within a mile of her without wanting to kiss every freckle on her face, edging downward, and—

"See?" she said softly, breaking into the fantasy. "You're thinking about it, I'm thinking about it. I don't think we can be alone without wanting more." The sadness in her voice told him she was already giving up. Again.

"Okay, so sex is fantastic for us. That's a bonus, isn't it? But we've done without it for the past few weeks and survived. You said you didn't know me," he challenged her. "So I'm here, Jules. Get to know me. We have two weeks. Give me this time, Jules. Give us a chance before you give up!"

"I want to, Matt," she replied passionately, sounding choked, "but—"

"You're either giving us a chance or you're not. You stay or run away. I always thought of you as so brave, so strong," he mocked, giving in to the fury for a moment. "Give me these two weeks. While you're here, be with me, Julie. Fight for us! Show me you think we have something worth fighting for!"

Her mouth opened; she breathed through parted lips as she stared at him. "I don't know, Matt. I—"

"Well, I do know," he snapped, low. After a quick glance to see where Molly was—she'd found a little girl to play with, looking at each other's prizes—he turned back, his whole body red-hot with anger. "You say too much has been left unsaid. You say it's always you reaching out. Well here I am, talking. I'm reaching out, Julie. I don't know if what we have is worth saving at this point, but damn, I want to know. But I can't do it alone, Julie. I need you to be with me!"

"I know exactly what you mean." She turned her face. "It's exactly how I've felt for the past six months."

"All right, I admit it. I took you for granted when I shouldn't have," he snarled, making her jump. "But how the hell can I fix it if you won't even try?"

"Maybe I'm tired of trying."

"So why the hell are you still here? Why are you helping me? Why do you look at me like it's not over?" He felt as if he'd run a marathon; he couldn't breathe. "Why can't you keep your hands off me?"

She gulped and closed her eyes. "I don't know, Matt. *I don't know!*" she cried, sounding wretched. "All I know is, when I needed you, you weren't there."

"So you actually wanted time alone with me?" His voice was still dark, still hard. "You never once asked me to stay when I said I had to go." Challenging her to say what he could see she was hiding.

"How *the hell* can you doubt that I wanted it?" The words shocked him; it was almost a snarl, a tigress with flashing eyes leaping at him. "I'm still here, Matt. I'm always here, always waiting for you. I've been coming last to other people and work and problems for months on end, but I'm still *here*. You're the one who's never here, never with me!"

Matt sucked in air like a diver with the bends. "What?"

"That's the worst of it. You don't even

notice," she all but yelled at him. "I *know* they all need you. I know you have to support your mother, you had to save McLachlan's. Maybe it was necessary to spend time with Elise on making and selling the converter. I know you need to bond with Molly. But no matter what, it's always the same. Your mother or someone at work or from the media calls, and you're out of here. Someone else or something else needs you and gets your time while I wait. I've been there for you every time you needed me, from your father's death right down to this week— but what about when I needed you, Matt?" She made a small, choking sound, and her cheeks flushed dark.

"I needed you when it looked like The Belles was going under, and I could lose my work visa as well as my job. I needed you when all my friends found men to love! I was happy for them, but for weeks and months I was so lonely I cried myself to sleep, *and you weren't there.*

"I needed you to fight for me after the engagement party, to convince me I was worth it, and work out our problems. I needed you to spend time with me to convince me you didn't love Elise. I needed you to kidnap me to spend time with *me,* not help you with Molly. I needed you to see that yesterday was your last chance with *me,* not just Molly!

"You're such a white knight…but I'm tired of waiting for you to see me. I've given up waiting for you to rescue me." Tears of fury or emotion flashed up in her eyes, but she dashed them away, glaring at him with her chin stuck out and her eyes red-rimmed. "I can't do this anymore. I can't give you another chance. I'll stay for Molly, but you have to accept it's over. I'm *tired,* Matt. I haven't got anything more to give."

The tigress had pounced, and torn him apart with claws unsheathed. She'd laid her heart at his feet, bared for him to see. At last he knew the real depth of Julie's problems with him.

He felt devastated. He felt like the world's biggest jerk.

No wonder she doubted his love. No wonder she didn't believe his words. He'd never wanted to hold her more than now, but that wouldn't help either. He didn't have a single idea what would help…but as she'd said, she was *here,* his beautiful miracle, his loving Julie. And he'd all but destroyed her, starved her love…and yet she was here.

How could he *not* have seen she was drowning? Exhausted, falling down emotionally, neglected too long without family to cover her back, without *him* to even notice, and yet still she was here, still giving to him when all he deserved was his ring thrown in his face.

Was there ever a woman like this one?

And a light shone in the darkness. She'd done nothing but give to him from the day they'd met, and he'd been grateful and adored her for it, but, lost in the mess his father had left and his mother's grief, he'd taken Julie's strength and courage and grace, and given only neglect and sexuality in return. In other words, he'd taken her love for granted.

It wasn't merely his turn to give; he had to *learn* to give.

"Hey, Matt, look, I won a tiger!"

Almost relieved to have a moment to think, he turned to his excited daughter bouncing toward them and conjured up a smile from somewhere in his devastated depths. "That's a real beauty, Molly," he said, barely even noticing that he was using Julie's words…or that sometime in the last minute, he'd taken Julie's hand in his, softly caressing her palm. He didn't know if Julie wasn't pulling away because she wanted his touch, or because she was just too tired to fight.

"It's enormous. You must have won from

the top shelf," Julie called to her, with an obvious effort.

"I did!" Molly yelled, bouncing some more. "Matt, come see what else I won!"

"Go to her," Julie's voice was almost a whisper. "I'm all right."

About to nod and thank her, in his mind came another "click." That was what Julie always said when someone else demanded his time or attention...and until now, he'd been grateful for her understanding, and had left her, resolving to make it up to her later.

But later had never really come. He hadn't given her much of anything apart from her engagement ring and the engagement party. Grand gestures, indeed, but it seemed he'd gotten it wrong both times. He had to learn to get it right.

She had that wilted-flower look that had haunted him from the night of their engagement party. She expected him to go—and she was right. He had no choice but to take care of Molly, but damn it, his heart was torn between the daughter he barely knew and the fiancée on the edge of walking away. He loved them both, and had blown it so badly with both.

"Let's go together," he said, smiling at her, praying to God he'd gotten it right for once, that she wanted the invitation.

Julie bit her lip, the indecision clear in her eyes.

"I've been a jerk, Jules, but I can't start to make it up to you if you aren't with me," he whispered. And he caressed her cheek, pushing back an errant curl, not with the pulsing sexuality that still blew him away even now, but with tenderness. "Please, Jules, come with me." He released her hand and held his out to her. Giving her the choice.

Like a sleepwalker waking to unfamiliar surroundings she stood up, with a tentative smile—but she didn't look at him or take his hand. With an effort he smiled back, and together they crossed the courtyard to where Molly waited to share her fun with them.

CHAPTER EIGHT

THERE was a delivery truck filled with things for Molly when they arrived back at the house, just as the sun was beginning to fall behind the hills in the distance. Molly was jumping out of the car as soon as the truck door opened and a grinning bald man in a blue uniform hopped down. "Well, I don't think I need to guess who this climbing gym is for, huh?"

"Me! Me!" Molly cried. "I'll show you where I want you to put it. Can you put it up? Cuz my dad's probably no good at making swings and stuff?"

The truck driver denied any responsibility for assembly, took his payment and almost tore down the driveway before Molly could rope him into more work. Julie all but fell onto one of the exquisite iron-lace chairs on the veranda. She geared herself up, ready to intervene between father and daughter; but she was so tired.

"Can I at least have a shot at putting it together?" Matt asked, his tone cheerfully indignant. "I am an engineer, you know, Molly."

Molly snorted. "That's on *boats*. What do you know about swing sets and see-saws? I bet Julie could put it together better than you." She sent Julie a hopeful look.

"I think Julie's done enough for us for one day, Molly," Matt said, but without the weary rancor of yesterday. "And I think she deserves her surprise before we get into putting up your stuff."

"Yeah, all right," Molly grumbled, but with a glimmer of a cheeky grin. "Where is it, anyway?"

"In the trunk." Matt popped the trunk, and Molly almost dived in head-first to grab whatever it was they'd bought for her.

Julie watched them, feeling as if she stood on uncertain ground. This present couldn't be a reaction to her outburst at the fun park; they'd come straight home from there. Matt had to have bought it earlier.

Molly and Matt, looking like twins born years apart, emerged from the trunk with a box each and matching grins. "Surprise!" Molly yelled, waving something around. "It's gonna be great. Close your eyes and promise not to peek!"

Despite her exhaustion, Julie couldn't hold back a grin as she closed her eyes. "Wake me up if I fall asleep," she said, yawning.

"There won't be much of a chance of that, trust me," Matt laughed.

The sound of his laughter rippled through her body like sweet rain on parched ground. It came so rarely…but this past day, it had seemed far more natural.

She hadn't realised how much she'd missed it, the simple sound of his happiness, until she heard it again.

She got his point almost immediately, when the happy arguments and hammering sounds broke into every second moment of peace. "No, you don't put it there!"

"Well, where would you suggest, since I'm only an engineer and wouldn't have a clue how to work these things?"

More banging and hammering.

"*Duh,* Matt! Look at the paper that came with it. No, here! See, you're putting D into F instead of G!"

"You'd be right if I was holding D, kid, but I'm holding M."

"Oh." Paper rustled. "Does M go into G?"

"Yeah, see? Right here."

More hammering, with Matt obviously

watching Molly attempt to hammer something in. "Watch it, Molly, careful of your thumb."

"Yeah, whatever. You're in my way!"

More hammering.

"Okay, Molly, this is where it gets harder. It's my turn now."

"Okay. I'm thirsty. Can I get a soda?"

"Water or juice," Matt said, sounding distracted. More hammering sounds followed his words. "You've had enough soda for today."

Again Molly grumbled, but she swished past Julie into the house. She seemed to accept Matt's dictum without argument...and Julie wondered why Molly had knuckled under so well within a day.

Maybe the same reason I did, she thought wryly. *We just can't say no to him. Neither of us can resist him for long.*

It was obvious how much Molly loved her father, how much she'd needed time with him, even if she hadn't wanted to at first.

Matt cursed as, by the squeaking sounds, he was evidently trying to pull something up or make it stick together. Julie tried hard not to laugh. He swore again, and this time she knew she was grinning. When he walked in foreign territory, fell down and picked himself up again, he wasn't the intimidating Matthew McLachlan, but just a man who wasn't giving up.

"Damn this stupid—" The words cut off as Molly swished past her again, and called out some more advice to him. "Yes, okay, Molly, thanks," he said, trying to sound like he had everything under control.

This was so *cute*. Matt was so adorable when he was trying to be the family man.

"Don't get cranky, Matt. I'm back now. I can help," Molly said cheerfully, affection for her father in every syllable.

She wondered if her love for Matt was as obvious as Molly's, and if so, if Matt could see it so clearly. Was that why he wasn't giving up?

What did it matter? She'd known all along that her love for Matt wasn't the issue. And the fact that he was trying so hard now to keep them together, that he'd gotten angry enough to fight for her, felt like balm soothed over an untreated, closed-over wound: too little too late. And though he'd reached out, though he'd talked to her, almost all of it was about Molly. What would happen when Molly was gone?

"You gotta hurry, it's gonna be dark soon and you won't get to my stuff!"

"That's what floodlights are for, Molly. Your

stuff will be up tonight or I lose the title of Best Biological Parent Ever."

"Yes!" Molly cried, and again, despite her gloomy thoughts, Julie smiled. These two were meant to spend far more time together than a few days every year. Matt was born to be a father in reality, not just when his ex needed a babysitter.

"Look, Julie! Ta-da!"

She opened her eyes, and despite her bitter thoughts, her whole face broke into a smile. She got to her feet and walked the four steps to her gift, her heart overflowing with a simple happiness she hadn't known in months.

"Welcome to the first step in making this Julie and Matt's house," Matt said when she touched the canopy of the old-fashioned double-seated porch swing. Molly was dancing around her, asking did she like it, did she like it, didn't she love it and wasn't it great. "I guess I don't have to ask if you like it."

"You…you bought this before I told you…?" Mindful of Molly's presence, she let the sentence trail.

Matt didn't need an interpretation. "Yes," he said gruffly. "You were right last night. Molly was right. This isn't just not *your* home—it isn't mine, either. I never noticed it before."

Too busy working, they both thought, but didn't say.

Molly, clearly tired of the conversation, said, "Can I go put up my posters, Matt? I'll be real careful and won't make a mess."

"Sure—they're yours, Molly. Don't worry about mess. It's your room, put them where you want."

"Hahoo!" she screamed, and bolted up the stairs.

When they were alone, Matt said, "I want you to know this swing is yours, no matter what happens with us."

"It looks good here," she said slowly.

"Better than the iron lace stuff, at least. I want to make this a home," he went on, and though he didn't repeat the "Julie and Matt's house," he didn't have to. She could feel his nearness, sense his longing to touch her. It was in every syllable. "You shocked me last night. I'd never realised how much I'd become like Dad until I thought about it. Just because I wasn't like him—" he paused and then continued, sounding as if he was taking nasty medicine "—just because I wasn't like him in being unfaithful, I thought that meant I was a better man."

Julie gasped and turned to face him—close,

so close, and his beautiful face distorted with bitterness and unhealed pain. "Matt…"

He shook his head, putting a finger to her mouth. "I made the mistake of thinking his affairs were what hurt my mother the most." He took her hand in his, his finger still on her mouth, his eyes deep and serious on hers. Asking nothing, just giving. "I've handed Elise and Brad Gardiner the reins with McLachlan's until—for the next couple of months. I'm available by phone for emergencies, but that's all."

She couldn't tear her gaze from his, could barely hold back from taking that last step and wrapping her arms around him in comfort, if not in thanks. What could she say? This was a massive step for Matt, changing the habits of his adult life—changing work hours, telling her the things not just close to his heart but what made him the man he'd become. She didn't need to ask if he was making the sacrifices for her sake; she knew it was. For the first time in a long time, she knew he was putting her first.

"Matt…" She shook her head. Words had always come easily to her…until now when she needed them most. "Don't do this all for me." *I don't know if it's worth it.*

The finger, still on her mouth, moved gently, and she quivered inside. "What if it's not just for you?" he murmured. "What if it's for me, too? What if it's for a boy who got lost between an absent father and a mother too wrapped up in her pain to see her son and didn't know who he was? What if it's for a man who never knew goofing off could bring more peace and contentment than any multimillion-dollar deal? What if you're making me the man I was meant to be, but I never knew until you showed me all the things I wasn't?" Finally his finger moved; his palm cupped her cheek. "What if I've been happier in this one day than I've ever been, because I'm finding out who I really am? What if I like making swings and picking out posters and books and goofing off with my family?"

Helpless, all she could do was look at him. She felt like a child, too, a girl lost in her first crush—or was it seeing a beginning when she'd only expected an ending? Beautiful, lovely *what ifs* that could change her life as well as his…if only they lasted beyond a day.

"Don't say it, Jules. I know." He smiled and stepped back. "Try the swing, and think about it. I'll check on Molly's progress. Back in five."

Julie sat on the swing's padded cushion and absently began rocking. He hadn't needed to tell her to think about it; she couldn't think about anything else. No pretty words today, but truth so raw and shining, dismissing how they impressed her was impossible.

What if I'm finding out who I really am?

If only she could trust in this change....

Her phone rang at that moment. "Hello?" she said vaguely, thinking, wishing...

The rapped-out questions shattered the lovely bubble of hope she'd been floating in and landed her smack-bang back in reality.

Matt whistled very softly as he ran back down the stairs. Molly was better than fine, she'd told him to go away, she was *busy* getting her room right, and music—very loud music—was keeping her company. He was obviously in the way, so he ran back to Julie. Maybe he could try out the new swing...and take time out, just sitting beside Julie, and talking. They could order pizza and ice cream, or something else Molly liked, and have a picnic out here. Then they could make the kiddie gym together by the brightness of floodlights.

Goofing off. Enjoying a warm, almost-summer night with his family. Hoping he could make Julie as happy as he was right now, no pretty words or touching, just being together.

Once she was off the phone, anyway. As he turned the corner of the house to the side terrace, he could hear her talking, and hung back in case she didn't want him to hear. But the bewildered distress in her voice was louder than the words she spoke. He moved closer.

"I…I don't. I…who told you that? I…I don't understand…why is this relevant? My past is nobody's business but mine. No, I don't have a comment on how this could possibly affect Matt, Ms. Whittaker. I don't have any more to say. Goodbye."

She hiccupped as she disconnected, and he saw the tracks of tears falling down her cheeks. Matt stepped forward then. "You okay, Julie?" he said softly, his hand on her hair, caressing in gentle comfort.

She stared up at him, looking bewildered, betrayed. "They found Peter Blake. He…he sold the story—his version of the story. They're going to print it tomorrow. She asked me—" Julie hiccupped again, and shook her head. "She said I've become news through you," she whispered. "My private past has become…*entertainment*…because of you."

CHAPTER NINE

"I CAN'T take this anymore. She said...she asked..."

She sounded dazed, lost. Just as she had the night of their engagement party—and again Jemima Whittaker had ruined Julie's lovely day.

Holding in his initial reaction for her sake— the need to snatch the phone, call *Boston People Today* and scare the hell out of Whittaker— he sat beside her on the swing and put an arm around her. "Tell me what she said, Jules."

She shifted, as if his touch made her uncomfortable, but he didn't pull back. She'd accused him of not being there for her when she needed him. Well, he wasn't going anywhere this time. He tightened his arm, stroking her shoulder. "It's my business, too, Jules. I can't help you if you don't share."

"All right," she agreed slowly, her gaze hooded,

but she didn't pull away from his touch this time. "She asked if I meant it when I told Peter I loved him. If I'd come to you on the rebound." She blushed, exhaling hard. "She asked which of you was the better lover, *for the record.*"

And Matt saw red. "I'll deal with this." He pulled his cell phone from its holder and called the number he now knew well, after the exclusive given to the magazine for their wedding. "I want to speak to Ralph Emerson," he snapped when Emerson's PA answered the private cell number. "Tell him it's Matt McLachlan. Tell him if he doesn't speak to me now, I'll be speaking to my lawyer about pulling the exclusive on our wedding…and I'll be suing the legs out from under him."

Emerson was on in moments. Matt didn't allow him beyond the first wary greeting. "Jemima Whittaker is officially off our wedding piece—and you know why. I complained the first time, and accepted her assurances she wouldn't cross the line again. I'm not a forgiving man, Emerson. If that piece on my fiancée runs at any time before or after our wedding, your magazine is not only losing its exclusive, I'll litigate you into the next century."

He listened to the publisher babble for a few moments, then spoke in utter fury, with none of the freezing politeness he was famed for. "A respectable builder? You really should check your facts, Emerson. Blake—" he cut off an excited question "—I won't dignify that vulgar question with a reply. Blake is a con man. He was imprisoned for eighteen months two years ago for cheating old folks out of savings by making fake repairs to their houses. And since he was paroled, he's slipped out of the charges, but it's only a matter of time. He's on an official 'persons of interest' list across Australia. So if you run the piece, I have grounds to sue you into your magazine's early grave without answering a single question about my fiancée's supposed past."

He heard Julie suck in a shocked breath, and he gently caressed her shoulder again as he listened to Emerson's obvious panicked bluster.

"Do you think I give a damn what the public wants? You will pull the story on my fiancée, take Whittaker off the story and keep the watchdogs away from my family until the wedding day, or I'll gag you permanently. And you know I can."

He disconnected the line while Emerson was babbling apologies, and turned to Julie. "It's gone, Jules. Whittaker's off the story. You won't ever have to deal with her again."

She was staring at him in something between

shock and awe. "I've never seen you so angry. You've never shown me that side of you."

He grinned and winked. "And you're fervently hoping you never have to be on the receiving end of it?"

She almost smiled at that. "I couldn't believe it when she called. It was like a nightmare. She'd always been so pleasant before. But she thought— Peter turned the whole thing around, saying I'd ditched him for a rich man." She frowned deeply. "How did you know about Peter being in prison?"

"I hoped I'd never need to tell you this." He took her hands gently in his. "My father had you investigated, Jules. I only knew when I got the report after he died. In fact, I only found out that he knew about Molly after he'd died. He'd investigated every girl I ever brought home."

"Seeing if they were good enough to be potential brides of the McLachlan heir." Her tone was colourless.

"Yes."

Suddenly she smiled, in one of her lightning turnarounds of emotion, in her wonderful ability to find humour in most situations, especially about herself. "So, tell me, did they say I'm dangerous to your health and welfare?"

"Definitely." He spoke with mock fervor,

laying a hand over his heart. "You're bound to kill me before I turn forty."

Her brows lifted. "And still you proposed. You're an adventurous man, McLachlan."

No, he wanted to say, *just in love.* But it would only make her withdraw. So he said softly, "Tell me why this Peter issue was such a nightmare, Jules."

She frowned again. "Do I need to spell it out for you?"

"I think you do." He wound his fingers through hers. "Everyone gets dumped for someone else in their lives, even for their sister. So why is the idea of others knowing this one so horrifying?"

"You know the story," she said, her voice pure frost.

"I don't think I do—not the whole thing." When she tried to pull her hand away, he held fast. "Was Whittaker right? Do you still have feelings for the guy?"

"No! Yes!" she cried wretchedly, and his heart jerked. "The feelings for the first one don't just go away. I thought I loved him, Matt. I thought it was forever. And to find out he tried to hit on Veronica…and she had to be the one to tell me he'd also tried it on with three of my friends…" She lifted a white face to his. "The love may not ever have been real, but the betrayal and the hate and the distrust and the fear…it doesn't go away, don't you see? And I've been so alone…"

"Are we talking about him now or me?" he asked, low.

She closed her eyes. "It blurred when I heard about Elise from that Whittaker woman and not from you."

Matt closed his eyes, too. Every time he thought he'd reached the bottom, he found another layer of reasons why she'd pulled away. He cursed Peter Blake, but cursed his own silence most. So much damage to such a loving heart.

He leaned forward until his forehead touched hers. "I haven't even looked at another woman since the day we met. I can't think of any way to convince you of that, but it's the truth. I'm not him, Julie."

She moved a little, face to face, in a tentative caress. "I know you're not, Matt." Like a butterfly's fluttering landing, she put her fingers on his shoulder. "But secrets hurt and divide. They destroy trust. I trusted you, and when I found out so many things you never told me…and now this." She sighed, and as he opened his eyes, she started to move away from him, inch by inch. "I don't think I'm cut out for this life, Matt. I can't handle the interest in my past and present."

"It's over, Jules." He pulled her back to him, gently and slowly. "It's gone, and let's face it, sweetheart—Peter Blake was all they were going to find." His eyes twinkled. "You've led such a respectable life. It would have been a massive disappointment to my poor father."

Caught off guard, she chuckled.

He took her chin in his fingers, caressing. "You won't believe me now, but you'll learn to cope with it, to shrug it all off. Sticks and stones, etcetera."

But she sighed and moved out from his hand. "God help me if I had to do that, time after time. I didn't fight, Matt. I just...took it."

"I do understand the shock it's been to you, Jules. I've dealt with the garbage most of my life. I grew up knowing my family was news around here, and my private life was open to scrutiny. You learn to grow a tough outer shell. You learn which lies to ignore and when to attack."

"I don't want to get tough. I don't want to attack anyone," she whispered. "She took Peter's words as truth because you're rich. She fabricated an entire story from a kernel of truth, and I just sat there and listened and said no, no."

She looked at him, her frown deepening. "The past two days have been…intense. I need some time alone."

Wanting to cut through the layers of self-protection she was wrapping around herself, he willed some calm. "Of course. I'll order dinner in." He thought of his family picnic with a pang; obviously she wouldn't—

Why was he assuming she'd prefer a formal dinner in the house she hated than a picnic that would take her away from all the reminders of this ugly episode?

Ask.

"I was thinking along the lines of pizza and ice cream out here on the grass, and making Molly's kiddie gym together. I thought a bit more down time would do us all good. What do you think?"

In the act of rising to her feet, she turned her head, surprise written all over her face. "I think Molly would love it."

"But will you love it?" he pressed.

She blinked again. "I don't know, Matt."

He squelched the disappointment. Of course she didn't know. She'd been through a damn tough thirty-something hours. Not even two days, and she'd taken hit after hit. And still she was here. That was miraculous in itself.

He wouldn't pile on more pressure.

"If you need more down time, I can bring you room service in two courses—pizza and crème brulée ice cream, eaten straight from the carton with a plastic spoon, of course." He forced a grin he was far from feeling. "Saves on washing up, right?"

"Right." A pale smile, watery and tired, still had the power to make his day. The last rays of the day's sunlight touched her face. She looked about seventeen, sweet and shy, her bright-blue eyes glowing, her hair a mess of red spirals and her freckles standing out on unrouged cheeks.

And he damn well adored her so much he was hurting with it.

"I'm sorry, Matt," she said, sounding sad and awkward. "And thank you for what you did just now." The smile grew. "Remind me never to make you that mad. I don't think I could handle the ruthless businessman hiding beneath the man I—" She shook her head. "The man I thought I knew, anyway."

"It only happens when the people I love are threatened," he replied without thinking. Panic at her obvious withdrawal caused him to say the words the saner part of him knew she wasn't ready to hear again. "And only when the people in question deserve it."

She jerked to her feet. "I promise not to threaten them, then," she said, stiff as a waxwork. She held up a hand as he started to say something, anything, to bring back the connection they'd created today. "No, don't, Matt. Today's been—" She sighed. "I'm going for a walk. I need time out."

She left the house, still wearing the ketchup-stained shirt from the fun park, her hair spiralling about her face, but she seemed every inch the queen as she walked out—and every inch as distant.

Matt cursed, long and fervent. Why was it that he could bring a crumbling business multi-million-dollar contracts and save five hundred jobs, and he could bring a publisher to his knees with a few well-chosen comments, but he couldn't stop making blunders with the woman he loved?

CHAPTER TEN

IT WAS long after dark when Julie returned, but the floodlights made the entire yard of the house seem drenched in so much brightness, it was a wonder the neighbors weren't complaining—and about the noise levels, too. By the sounds of it, Matt and Molly were hammering the kiddie gym into place, with all the same funny arguments as this afternoon.

Strange that a two-hour walk could do nothing to clear the turbulence in her mind and heart, but a load of banging and cheerful insults could make her feel as if she'd come home. But then, as her family could attest, Julie Montgomery was not your average woman.

Neither was Matt, if he'd spent the happiest day of his life hammering at swings and barfing at fun fairs.

She could just imagine Scott's or Jason's reactions if she told them. *No wonder you're marrying the guy, he's as weird as you are.*

She smiled, thinking of all the weird ways her clan expressed caring, the tight-knit loving and fierce loyalty couched in cartoon terms and affectionate insults. She missed them all so much.

Still she smiled as she walked over to where father and child were arguing about where one of them had put the turnkey. "Hey. Sounds like you two are about as happy as pigs in mud."

Molly's face screwed up in indignation, but Matt laughed. "She did it." He pointed at his daughter.

"He lost it!" Molly retorted with more heat than originality.

Julie laughed. "I think he also lost his watch."

Matt frowned at her, then checking the time, muttered, "Oh, da—heck, your mom won't be happy with me if she hears you've been awake until nine."

"Matt was gonna swe-ear," Molly sang, a cheeky look on her face. "You are *so* in trouble. Whatcha gonna give me for not telling Mom?"

"You got enough today." Matt laughed and swatted in the direction of her butt. "So scoot, kid."

Julie lifted her brows. "Your father means

after your bath, of course. I'll go run it for you."
She turned toward the house, still smiling.

"I like the purple bubbles in it," Molly yelled.

It was almost an hour before Matt closed the
door on his sleeping daughter. He'd read to
Molly after Julie sorted out a pyjama crisis.
Molly utterly refused to wear a top and pants
that didn't match. He looked at Julie and leaned
against the door, heavy-eyed with weariness.
"What a day."

"And it's not over yet, unless you want to
lose your Best Biological Parent Ever title."
She swept a hand in the direction of the
backyard.

He groaned as he headed down the hall. "I
don't know how Kirsten does it full-time. She's
a handful, isn't she?"

"You're not used to it, is all," she said as she
followed him. "I always feel the same way after
a full day with…" She bit her lip, but the tears
rushed up anyway. "Felt the same way after
minding my nieces and nephews."

Oh, help, her voice had gone all thick.

And of course he heard it. He swung back to
her, concern etching his brow. "You okay?"

She shrugged, unwilling to put him through
the wringer of her emotions yet again. She was
worn out with it herself, and she was used to it.

"It's been a crazy couple of days, that's all. And Molly's the same age Miranda was when I left Sydney. She's eleven now…"

"And you haven't seen her in almost two years. You've only seen your mom and dad once since then, and that was a year ago." He came to her, putting his hands on her shoulders. "They'll be here soon, Jules."

She couldn't leave it unspoken. "Matt…"

A hand lifted, putting a finger to her mouth again. "Don't say it, Julie. Postpone the wedding if you have to, but don't say it's over. Don't say you don't love me anymore. I can't believe it. I couldn't stand to believe it."

The words were as real and raw as the look in his eyes. The pain felt like tiny barbs under her skin. She shivered.

"Go home if you have to, sweetheart. Go see your family. Take time out. God knows you deserve it. I'll handle the press, say the wedding's postponed." The hands on her slipped beneath the loose shirt, caressing her bare skin, and she felt herself flush with the desire never far from the surface. "Go first class. I'll book it for you. Rest, sleep, spend time with them. I won't call you. I'll give you time and space. Think or don't think, but don't end it, Jules. Not now. Not yet."

His touch was hypnotic, drawing her into a tidal pool of emotion and need. Her mind emptied of everything but truth. "I'm so homesick, Matt. I want to go home, but at this point it won't solve anything. I'll stay for now."

His hands slipped down her back, pulling her close. "Are you falling again?" he murmured into her hair. "Landing in that puddle?"

She nodded, her lips brushing his throat and shoulder.

"That's my Julie," he whispered kissing her forehead, her nose. "I'm falling, too, Jules. I'm off the sidelines for good. I'm on this adventure with you this time, mud on my face and all."

She felt the roughness of his bristled jaw, and realised she'd moved her body right against him, drinking in his scent, his skin, his warmth. "I wish…"

"I know, Jules, I know. This should have been happening months ago. But I was a jerk. You told me and showed me, and waited for me, but still I let you do all the falling. I wasn't even there to pick you up. But I'm here now." He kissed her ear, and she moaned. "I'm here. I'm not going anywhere. You mean too damn much to me."

"Matt, Matt," she whispered, aching for his kiss, his touch…

He cupped her face in his hands. "No, baby. Not yet. Wanting you is driving me crazy, but you were right, we did everything backward. I'm getting it right this time." He led her down the stairs to the blanket outside and gently laid her down. With a quirky grin he flopped beside her and, resting on one elbow, said, "I guess I either get up very early tomorrow, or lose the Best Biological Parent hat, but now it's your time, our time." He grew serious as he added, "I wouldn't blame you if you don't believe me, but from now on there'll always be your time, Jules. There'll always be our time."

He was right…she didn't believe it, no matter how she yearned to. But it had only been two days, and even the most committed workaholic could give up two days. If he gave her tomorrow and the next day, she might begin to believe.

Maybe in a few years she might trust that it was forever.

"So let's begin," he said, for once missing the emotions she knew had to be reflected in her eyes. "Hi, I'm Matt McLachlan, and I'm going to be the best kisser you'll ever know in your life."

She choked on unexpected laughter. So her predictable Matt was going for the unpredictable. She'd never have guessed they'd be here, lying beneath the warm, wind-tossed stars, playing a getting-to-know-you game months after they'd become lovers, weeks before their wedding. "Hi," she managed through the lingering chuckles. "I'm Julie Montgomery, expat Aussie who's saving for a trip home." She put out the hand her head wasn't resting on. "And I'm very interested to know why you think you'll be the best kisser I'll ever know."

"I'm a time traveler," he said seriously as he shook her hand. "You're going to tell me that in exactly four and a half minutes."

She giggled again, jerking her hand back to cover her mouth.

He grinned. "So tell me about yourself, Julie Montgomery, expat Aussie. What brings you to Boston? What are you doing with your life? What are your hopes and dreams, besides throwing me down on the blanket and kissing me in four minutes and nine seconds?"

Caught in the wonder of this new charm, she wondered if she could even wait that long—but she was finding such relief from the unrelenting stress of the past weeks in this game, she went along with it. She began to tell him about herself as if she'd met him at a party or in a bar.

"I'm twenty-nine. No, really, I am—" she chuckled when he snorted "—and I've been here four years now. My dad's an aeronautical engineer with QANTAS, so my flight here was cheap. I wanted to see more of the eastern states, fell in love with this place, so here I am. At the moment I'm a general assistant—you could say a phone-girl-cum-gofer—at The Wedding Belles, the complete-wedding-package business in beautiful downtown Boston. I like the job and love the women I work with, but one day I fully intend to become a world-famous photographer—"

"Hey, hold the phone," he protested when she was about to go on. "You've never told me that before. Are you serious?"

She pulled a face at him. "I thought we'd just met, Mr. Kisser of a Lifetime."

"No, really. Are you serious?"

Caught off guard by the intent look on his face, she nodded. "Well, it was always my dream, anyway. It's a bit ambitious, I know, to say I'll be world-famous…"

"Do you have any examples of your photography here with you?"

Self-conscious, she shrugged. "Not here in your house, but at my apartment, I do."

"Shots of what? The best views in America?"

"No, I like taking candid pictures of people, but from all around the world. I've been taking shots of whatever fascinated me from the time Mum and Dad gave me my first camera when I was eleven." She felt herself blush. "I lug a boxful of the things with me wherever I go."

"Show me, Julie."

"What, now? They're not here," she joked, to hide her embarrassment.

"Tomorrow, then." He still looked so serious. "You said I took you into my world. Now it's time I walked into yours. Go back to your apartment in the morning and lug your box here." Softly, gently, he pushed errant curls from her face. "Trust me with your secrets, Julie," he murmured, and the word *secrets* didn't sound wrong or horrible; he sounded like a friend, a conspirator. "I want to know them all."

"All right," she whispered back, but she shivered. Wondering why she'd never trusted Matt with this secret, this silly, unimportant secret before.

Wondering even more why now, of all times, she'd told him, and agreed to show him. Feeling as if it was a test she'd laid for him to pass or fail.

And maybe it was.

Matt pretended to check his watch. "You have exactly forty-two seconds before you throw me down on the blanket and ravish me. Just to stick to the timetable, you know." His eyes twinkled; he winked at her.

He was lightening the atmosphere every time it got remotely heavy, as if he knew how much she could take before she needed to laugh again. Who'd have known this side of Matt existed inside the inventor, the ruthless businessman, the driven workaholic?

What if I'm finding out who I really am?

The question haunted her, teased her with its sweet promise. Oh, how she wanted it to be true...

"Ten...nine...eight..."

She laughed again. But when he said, "Lift off," she threw him down. Lying over him, she looked into his smiling eyes and whispered, "I think you just might be the best kisser I've ever known—though you have serious competition from Artie Ashton, my year-seven-class crush."

Matt grinned. "Oh, yeah? Bet Cindy O'Malley, the cheerleader from my eighth-grade football squad, was better than him. I almost ran away with her."

"Oh, really? Well maybe we should introduce them, let them kiss each other, and leave us to it." She lowered her mouth to his.

CHAPTER ELEVEN

If Julie knew one thing, it was that she didn't want to go back to the anger and heartbreak and mistrust of the past weeks. It was time to open up to Matt, as he was opening up to her. It was time to give them a real, fighting chance.

Julie was sitting upright at the table in the formal dining room. She'd spent the morning at her apartment, catching up on overdue housework, and had checked in with The Belles for an hour and stayed for two, drinking coffee with revolving Belles as each found a little free time for her. Each had asked questions and offered advice, which all amounted to one thing.

You love him, Julie. Trust him now.

So here she sat with her big box of memories, ready to show him her most private hopes and dreams. Ready to fall, to take a leap and trust that he was there with her, because she didn't know if she could take landing in another emotional mud puddle.

Why she was sitting in the dining room, she didn't know at first. She hated every formal inch of it. But then she began planning how to make it warm and inviting as she waited for Matt to come back from dropping Molly off for her promised play date with Rose and Lily, and she knew why.

Part of her—a very big part—wanted this to work. The distrust was fading.

Matt was making sure of it.

"We need a few hours to ourselves," he'd written on the note she'd found when she arrived to an empty house. "Natalie's offered to take Molly bowling with the family tonight, and have pizza. Molly's 'over the moon' at finding girls who like the things she likes. I'll be back soon. P.S: I think I'm getting the hang of this multi-tasking thing!"

It seemed he was. In three days, he'd begun to open up to her, had won his daughter over, and unleashed his darker side to protect her, as well as showing her a self-deprecating charm she hadn't known he possessed. He had talents she hadn't been aware of until now....

Including the ability to make his fiancée fall

madly in love with him all over again within a couple of days, she thought wryly.

Fighting it had been futile. He'd opened the door a crack, and what she'd seen of the strong, funny, humble, lovable family man beneath the brilliant engineer, gentleman and hard-headed businessman made her fall head over heels a second time.

He'd become the man of her dreams again— and this time she hoped it was based on reality, because she didn't think she could go through this mess of pain and distrust and loss ever again.

Her heart was pounding even before she heard the car sweep up the hilly driveway and park in the garage behind the house. She could barely breathe when she heard his voice calling to her from the direction of the kitchen.

"I'm in the dining room." She sat and waited for Matt to find her.

As Matt walked through to the dining room, the room she rarely entered, he wondered why she'd chosen to use the room with the hated portrait of his forbidding grandfather hanging over them. Was this yet another test?

He stopped short of entering the room, thinking about today, how she'd put him off for almost seven hours, making him wait. Leaving The Belles before he arrived with

Molly for the play date. Making excuses to not see him, even after their beautiful time last night.

Well, he was tired of all this distrust. Hadn't he proven to her that he was changing, for her sake as much as his? It seemed for every step he took forward, she took two back, forcing him to chase her, over and over again. Didn't she consider how much it hurt him, even once?

That's the trouble, you never even noticed when I needed you.... I'm still here! I'm always here, always waiting for you....

Three days compared to months was minuscule. *Grow up, McLachlan. Be a man for her.* He set his jaw and forced a smile. Losing her wasn't an option, now or ever—and she'd soon know that.

He walked in—and lost his ability to breathe.

How did she do this to him without even trying?

She'd pulled her hair back in some kind of thick plait, with spirals falling down her neck and across her ears. The denim shorts and tank top she wore, sky-blue as her eyes, exposed soft white skin and all those tempting freckles—he'd kissed every one of them over the months they'd been lovers—and it made his mouth go dry and his heart hammer.

"Hi. You're beautiful." No rehearsal in the words, they came from the heart. He heard the ravenous hunger in the single word, and wondered if she'd accept it or back off.

"Hi," she said softly, her eyes darkening with the same desire. "You're not so bad yourself." She pushed out a chair beside her.

When he sat at the table, their thighs brushed, skin to skin in their summer shorts, and she didn't move away. A smell of green apples wafted from her hair, and the woman scent of lush sensuality filled his head and hardened his body. She smiled, her mouth curving in that mysterious woman-way that meant he was welcome—and wanted.

His mouth seemed filled with sawdust. He shifted in the chair, just to feel her skin touching his. So *long* since they'd done that… "So these are the photos?" he asked gruffly.

She didn't answer, and he saw she was having trouble breathing, just as he was. Her eyes had closed and her fists were curled over, as if to stop from reaching out—

And he realised that if she was killing him with all the stop-start, will-she-won't-she, he was doing the same to her. Despite external differences, he and Julie were two of a kind. They tortured each other as much as they wanted, needed each other. It just never went away, and probably never would. They had to work out the problems between them, or spend the rest of their lives grieving for what they'd lost.

He had to go slow and show her there was plenty worth saving.

"Jules?" he murmured huskily—but at the nickname, she moaned and twisted around to kiss him. She grabbed him and dragged him against her, taking it deep and hard, giving him all her held-in passion at once. And all his resolutions were lost.

"Matt, Matt," she moaned between kisses so hot he felt like they'd both burn to death…and what a way to go. "I've missed you, I've missed you, I've missed you. Touch me, I need you to touch me *now*."

That was his Jules, wanting him like hell and saying what was on her mind without fear—the Jules he loved and had missed like crazy over the past weeks—but even as he gave her what she demanded, a small voice inside him whispered that this wasn't the time.

Then her hands slipped under his shirt, and her mouth trailed down his throat, and he pushed the voice aside. All he could think of was her and lifting her onto the table and taking her then and there—

Then they were against the wall, kissing, touching, and she was whispering words he thought he'd never hear from her again, words of sweet passion saying she couldn't *stand* it, couldn't stand being near him and not having him....

His shirt was gone, hers was twisted across her body, and their hands and mouths reclaimed each other in passion, and what he hoped to heaven was eternal commitment—but while she whispered beautiful, sensual words, she didn't say the words he craved, the words she'd always said before. That she loved him and she always would.

At the thought, he felt something in him slow down. "Jules," he whispered roughly. "I want to know about the pictures."

Julie gasped, in and out, in and out, leaning against him. When she'd regained some control, she nodded.

He lifted her face to his and looked hard at her. "We have to sort this out, Jules. This see-sawing is driving us both crazy. There's no doubt how much we want each other, but the issue was never about that, was it?"

Slowly she shook her head. "I've accused you of messing things up with us, but last night, I realised it wasn't just you that held things back." She waved at the box on the dining table.

"Show me," he said, still husky and thick with want.

A slow smile curved her mouth again as she led him to the table and opened the very large box covered in wrapping paper of varying shades and patterns, and stickers from flights around the world. "It's something I've done all my life. I love photography. I've always wanted to do something in that field—but I can't do that within The Belles, since not only was Regina there first, she's far better than I am." She shrugged and smiled again. "I'd love to do something with it, though."

Matt watched her. She'd begun glowing with the first words; now she was shining like a lamp in a dark place.

"Here, see?" And she opened the first box.

Half an hour later he'd only gone through about twelve photos, he was so absorbed in each new subject. "Where did you say you took this?"

She peered over his shoulder. "Um, hang on…yeah, that's a town called Rothesay on the Isle of Bute in Scotland." Her voice turned dreamy. "It's a beautiful place, wild and old, windblown and untamed, with old Pictish forts and standing stones, and hedgerows by farms older than the European history of Australia. I'd love to go back."

He frowned, studying the photo. "But why did you take this shot just here? The walls are falling down."

Julie chuckled. "The castle was burned down in the seventeenth century by enemies of the royal Stuart family. It's now a tourist attraction. Once you go in, it's like you walk back in time to a council of war between the Highland clans, fighting each other or fighting England. So many places in Europe are like that. You can find tumbledown houses and broken castles that make you feel as if you're Alice, fallen through the rabbit hole to be suddenly transported to another time and place. It's magical."

He shrugged. "I'm no photographer, but I don't see anything magical about a broken wall and all that rain."

"That wasn't why I took the shot. Look at the kids in front of the wall."

He looked, and looked again. "Oh." He heard his own voice, drawing out the word with wonder.

It was a great postcard show at first glance: a tumbledown castle wall, a moat and the remains of what appeared to be an inner bailey or chapel, in pouring rain. But before it, a smaller reality: two children, probably no more than five, doing what looked to be a victory dance around a massive mud pie topped by two flags: a sad-looking Union Jack and a St Andrew's Cross drooping in the wet weather. The children were drenched, muddy and under-dressed, but their arms were raised high, and as a bolt of lightning had crossed the sky, Julie had captured their faces lifted to the heavens, whooping with the innocent joy of living.

"They're having a really good time, aren't they?" he whispered, as if they'd hear him and vanish if he spoke aloud.

"Yes. I saw them, and had to take the picture. I remembered when I loved dancing in the rain around mud pies."

He laughed. "The little girl doesn't seem to care that she's showing her underwear."

Julie chuckled. "Do you remember caring about where your knickers were when you were four and doing a celebration dance around the best mud pie in the world?"

"I wouldn't know. I didn't do mud pies—at least not until this morning. Molly and I played under the hose today and made a mess of the garden." He grinned at her, remembering coming into the house covered in dirt, but with Molly's hand in his. "And what are knickers? Is that another Australian word?"

"Another word for underwear." Julie laughed with him. "Um, actually, I think it's English, and we took it. We're like that, you know. All descended from thieves and convicts...and mud-pie makers."

Their shared laughter sounded silver and golden to him.

He pored over the next picture, an old man looking radiant as he tried to windsurf in Fiji. "You should go into business."

Julie squirmed a bit. "I've thought about it, but I've got the best friends in the world, and The Wedding Belles is a fantastic place to be, very energetic and fun."

Matt noted she didn't say, I love my job.

The wheels started turning in his head...but the warning beat insistently beneath. *Make sure this time. Don't keep secrets from her.*

So he looked at the next photo...and he sucked in a breath. Staring, unable to take his eyes from the subject of the shot—not the scenery, but the *life.*

A terrace house—or a slim, tall house that looked as though it ought to be a terrace house, but standing alone. Flat-roofed in a shimmering haze of coming dusk, dust motes flying around it, it stood like a small pinnacle of light and truth amid a swirl of riotous colour. And yet it was only a backdrop for the reality.

A woman stood in the opening doorway in

the traditional burq'a and veil, her form lost apart from the shape of her down-turned head. She watched her husband, who tenderly held her hand.

The young man's face was aglow with reverent love.

"What's wrong? Say something," she whispered, breaking into his trance, and he started. How long had he been sitting there, lost?

"You took this?" he whispered back.

"We were just passing in a bus from Marrakech, and I saw it." A self-conscious shuffling of her feet beneath the chair. "I always kept my camera ready to shoot in those days."

"Jules—" he shook his head, still staring "—I want to walk right into this picture. I want to meet these people." He spread his hands across the photos he'd seen. "I want to go to all these places. You make them more real than any travel agency I've visited." He held a hand out. "More."

For the next half-hour, that was the only word he could say, again and again, apart from "Where is this?" She handed him one shot after another, all filled with life stories captured in a moment. Making the world such a small place by the humanity of each face, no matter its colour or faith displayed by veil or nose ring or robes and shaved head. A celebration of...of—

"That's it for this box," she said eventually, when he'd viewed over a hundred shots. "I have others at home with Mum and Dad, but these are my favourites."

"You take them all with you?"

She lifted a shoulder, looking tense, uncomfortable. "Wherever I go. They…they comfort me."

He nodded, gazing at a shot of a pair of barefoot newlyweds in Bali, wearing island gear, the groom lifting his bride in the air in wild triumph, the bride laughing with joy and love.

"I can see why they give comfort," he said, laying it aside for yet another look at the one of two kids of about ten or eleven locked in ferocious battle in the middle of a true medieval village in Alsace, France, complete with wooden swords and what looked like tin-foil shields and helmets. "They're…they're an affirmation of life."

"Yes." The word held a gentle wonder. "You understand."

He looked up and smiled at her, wanting to ask why he wouldn't, but half-afraid. "Who couldn't understand? These are—" he scrambled for the right word "—luminous. Alive." He hesitated. "These would make a marvellous professional portfolio, Jules…or compiled into one of those coffee-table books."

The expression of gentle eagerness dissipated from her face. "You're just being nice." She began collecting the photos scattered over the table, filling the box with them.

It was now or never; he had to pass this test to break through the barrier she probably didn't even know she'd erected against him. "I've never lied to you, Julie. I've never once said something I didn't mean. You have an amazing talent. Why are you wasting your life as a general girl Friday for The Belles?"

Her hand stopped halfway between them, reaching out for another photo, frozen there. Her gaze on his was so crystal clear, beautiful in its wistfulness he ached. "I have to work. This is something I do for the love of it."

"That's obvious," he said with absolute sincerity. "The interest in the people, the love for what you do shimmers in every photo." He met her eyes. "Being able to capture those moments the way you do, in the places you've been, is a rare art. Many excellent professional photographers catch a perfect waterfall or a beautiful sunset, but you capture moments in time that won't come again. Like the shots on the covers of *Time Magazine*." He went on, even as she lifted a hand. "People ought to be able to see the world the way you do."

Her lovely, made-for-smiles-and-kisses mouth fell open. "You're comparing my little memories with the cover shots in *Time Magazine*?"

He held his ground, and her gaze. "Yes. I am. You could make a really good career for yourself using these—either in books, or…"

"I like working for The Belles," she said, sounding confused, almost scared.

"I know, Jules." He gathered her hands in his. "They're your friends—"

"No. I love being part of The Belles. It's where I want to be, where I belong. It was right, from the first moment I walked in. I can't expect you to understand."

Matt laughed and tweaked her nose, as he always had when she was being absurd. "I work in a place my grandfather built and my father carried on, and you don't think I can understand?"

"Then don't push me to leave," she cried suddenly, startling him. "I love my friends, and being part of the life and energy of it all. Seeing a wedding created from nothing but wishes…seeing the bride and groom and families so happy. It—" she blushed "—it's like a constant reaffirmation of life and happy endings. And The Belles have the perfect photographer already. Regina. And I'd *never* try to compete with her. Not only is she far more talented than me, she's the best friend I have!"

"You don't have to try to take Regina's job or leave The Belles." Seeing now that the idea that had come to him a few minutes ago would be more than just good for her but *perfect,* sudden excitement rippled through him. "Add to it."

She frowned up at him. "What?"

He smiled down at her, still holding one hand in his, loving that she was allowing the touch, because it wasn't sexual, it was tender, friendly. "Have you ever thought that you have a hundred unique honeymoon destinations in these pictures? Have you thought of making posters of these pictures, and showing them to brides and grooms to see what they want, or where else they could go besides Florida or Hawaii or the Caribbean? You could take a photography course if you want—but I think you've already graduated." He smiled. "So why not take a travel agent's course, and create a new aspect of the business? Be the honeymoon planner."

Julie froze completely, staring at him, her breath slow and shallow. "I…I…"

Knowing the power of silence while someone digested a new idea, he waited. He'd done all he could. Now he waited for her to take the idea and run with it. It was the perfect job for Julie, using the creativity she'd hidden for so long—*why,* he had yet to discover—and staying with her beloved Belles.

Would she take it?

After what seemed forever, Julie squeezed his hand. "Matt," she breathed. "Do you really think I could do it?"

"I know you can. I already want to go to all these places, and see them through your eyes." He tipped up her chin with his free hand. "You made me look at life differently from the day we met. Now I want to see the world this way— with hope and joy and beauty and celebration. And if you're worried about The Belles finding this a threat, don't. I'm a businessman, Jules. They'll go for this. They'd be insane not to. It's the perfect completion to the business." He didn't back down, just held her shocked gaze and waited.

Slowly the stunned look left her face, and a shy, eager glow replaced it, growing until she was utterly radiant. "If I got a portfolio together…and a business plan to show them it could only enhance what they have now…"

"Exactly." He grinned at her, unable to stop it. She was so *beautiful* with the shimmering excitement and knowledge that yes, she could do this. "You still have plenty of time off to get it done. Present it to them when you get back. I could help if you—"

"No. I think I need to do this on my own." She focused on him, her eyes pleading. "You gave me the idea, and I'm so grateful for that, but the rest has to be mine."

"I understand," he said, to cover the crushed hope that they could work on this together. "And it leaves me free to spend time with Molly. But I'm here if you need me for any aspect of the business side, research, marketing…I did all that with the water converter, you know."

"Mmm…thanks…" She was sorting out pictures, pushing them around on the table at varying angles. "If I take digitals of my older shots and add them to my current files, I could make a PowerPoint presentation, with spreadsheets showing the possible exponential growth of business by not sending clients to our favoured travel agencies. And then there's the bank to convince. We'd need to make changes to the building…"

She grabbed the day planner she always had in her bag and started making notes.

"If you have any trouble with the bank—"

Then he closed his mouth. She'd said it had to be hers; he understood that need. In any case, she wasn't talking to him; she'd forgotten he was there. And while he smiled for her enthusiasm, glad he'd helped her find the path to a career that would keep her in Boston, for the first time he began to understand what she'd meant by being alone even when he was there.

Now obviously wasn't the time to mention his other idea, or she'd be lost in possibilities right past their supposed wedding day.

"I'll leave you to it. I have work I can catch up on," he said, wondering if she even heard him. Wondering if she'd felt as alone as he did now, when he was neck-deep in plans to create the water converter, taking it for granted she wouldn't want to know.

"Wait," she cried, holding out a hand to him. Suddenly *with* him, one hundred percent. "I want your opinion. I think twenty shots will be more than enough for a thorough presentation. Which are the best to impress the bank as well as The Belles, do you think?"

That was his Julie—always sensing others' hurt and doing something about it. He grinned and sat back down. "Well, since you ask, the Arabic one and the Scottish island place are both unusual honeymoon destinations."

She nodded as she found those shots and put them front and centre. "Of course I'd have to work out the best times for honeymoons there…"

His phone began the blooping tune they both knew too well. A call from McLachlan's. The familiar call to arms.

The smile vanished from her face.

"I have to answer, Jules. I said only to call in emergency." Of course she wouldn't be happy about it, but she'd understand—she always had. It wasn't as if he'd answered a hundred calls lately.

"Of course, go ahead." Her gaze returned to her photos—then she pushed her chair back. "I'll leave you to it." She walked into the kitchen.

He flipped the phone open—but the hope that he could sort it out in moments ended before he'd heard the first sentence.

Walking out to find her a few minutes later, he wondered why he felt so stupidly nervous— this was a big deal. "I have to go, Jules, sorry. One of the motor companies we're dealing with has demanded my presence at a meeting we scheduled at the plant this afternoon. I wanted to leave Elise and Brad to do it, but he said if I'm not there the deal won't go ahead."

She was stirring a mug of coffee. "Of course. It's fine."

But it wasn't. She didn't turn to him with the old, reassuring smile.

"I'll be back in a few hours, Jules," he said, hoping to see her smile, to feel the understanding he'd relied on since McLachlan's began heading toward receivership. "We can work on your presentation then."

She kept stirring the coffee long after the sugar was mixed in. "Don't worry about it. I can do it on my own."

Her replies sent a shot of anger through him. It wasn't as if he'd called work, he *had* to go now. "I *want* to worry, Jules. I want to be part of it."

She gave a short laugh. "You are already. No matter what happens with this, you'll always be a part of it. So go, and don't worry about Molly. I'll look after her for you."

They were the words he'd been angling for— the words that, weeks ago, he would have taken at face value and thanked God for her and run.

Now all he heard was the bitterness threaded beneath the blanket reassurance. She was severing the connection he'd been making with her, her fragile trust cracking. And there wasn't a damn thing he could do about it.

"Jules," he said huskily, reaching out for her.

"Please don't take it personally. I have to go. This is really important."

"Of course it is. It always is." She shoved the mug away with enough violence to send hot liquid sloshing over the counter. She snatched up her bag and keys by the door, then went into the dining room. She shoved her precious photos willy-nilly into the box.

"What are you doing? Where are you going?" he demanded, but had a sinking feeling he already knew.

She wouldn't look at him. "I think I'll go bowling with Natalie and the family. Call me when you're back and I'll drop Molly off. I need quiet time to work out my proposal. I'll stay at home until it's done. You and Molly are doing fine now. You don't need me."

"I do need you! Damn it, Jules, don't do this to us," he growled as he followed her to the door. "I'm only asking for a few hours. Surely by now I've proven to you that—"

She turned on him, her eyes flashing. "*Two days,* Matt. Forty-eight hours is all you've given me after almost a year of putting McLachlan's first, last and always. I've had almost a year of your leaving me to wait for you *for a few more hours.* I haven't been second in your priorities—I've come dead last every time."

"Hell, Julie, that's ridiculous! I realise I left you alone for too long. But I've worked at change! Lately it's been all you—"

"Has it? *Has it?* Let's count it up, shall we? If we don't include the time with Molly, *for* Molly and for making you a good dad instead of the enemy, I think we're looking at a grand total of four, maybe five hours where it's been 'all me.' When Molly arrived, I was useful to you. I was worth the effort for a couple of days, until another work 'emergency' came up." She closed the lid over the box with a gentle snap that seemed louder than a thud. It sounded less angry than final. "I didn't want all your time and attention, Matt. I didn't always expect to come first. Just…just sometimes. I kept waiting for it, for you, but it never came until you knew I was leaving you. Then you gave me *four hours* before you ran back to work. To me this proves you never loved me, only what I could do for you—keep your home life together so you could run the business."

Matt stood rigid. Put that way, of course it sounded bad. *Really* bad. But—

She didn't wait for him to speak this time. "But in your mind, it's me that hasn't given us a chance. I'm supposed to understand that a self-important businessman who wants a McLachlan to sit in on a meeting or the deal's off is a real emergency. It's worth millions that neither you nor the company needs with all the deals you already have in the works, but that isn't the issue. Nobody but you can handle the meeting, just like nobody but you can run the place. You're indispensable. Don't worry, Matt. I get it. But I won't be the dispensable, disposable part of your world anymore. I won't be your satellite." With bitter mimicry she said, "Thanks so much, Julie. I'll make it up to you, I promise. I'll schedule it. It's called 'quality time.' Is one day per year enough for you, or would you like it in one-hour increments once a month?"

And while he tried to think of a single thing to say that could refute her belief, this time it was Julie walking out on him.

CHAPTER TWELVE

Twelve Days Later

"SO THAT'S the whole kit and caboodle, girls. That's what I want to bring to The Wedding Belles. I'll give you all time to think it over."

As Julie walked out of the conference room, she realised she'd expected to feel different. She'd thought she'd have tummy cramps and heart palpitations and all the clichés. Yet all she felt was quiet confidence. She'd put together a damn good proposal, complete with tentative bank approval. And if they didn't go for it, she knew she had enough to start up her own holiday business.

This new self-assurance was the gift Matt had given her—not just by giving her the honeymoon planner idea, but also in finding the strength to walk away.

She'd called the wedding off the night she

left the house. And she'd only seen Matt once since then, this morning, when he'd brought his daughter to say goodbye before her flight back to Florida.

And while Matt was gentle and polite, and had asked only for a CD of her photos, which she assumed was to remember her by, Molly wouldn't look at her, had barely spoken a civil word to her. She'd called Matt Dad the whole time, loving and somehow defiant. Showing Julie whose side she was on.

Julie couldn't let it matter. Of course Molly sided with her dad. Why wouldn't she? Julie'd only been part of Molly's life for a few days. It wasn't as if it could do the child permanent damage. It wasn't as if she really mattered to Molly, or would for long.

As for Matt, he hadn't called her, hadn't asked to talk. He didn't want to try to salvage their relationship or win her back. She'd been right all along. He hadn't done whatever it took to make her love him again. And she was *glad* of that, she thought fiercely, *glad!*

Seeing him in the newspapers daily—seeing *herself* there as the reporters discussed all the possible whys and wherefores of the breakup— gave her the impetus to cancel her subscription. She refused to talk to anyone about Matt, except her family or The Belles. Everyone else was suspect. They could be from the press.

But within ten days the excitement had died down. Somebody famous had been seen at a drug den, another was having an affair with her married director, and, thanks be to heaven, Julie's love life was no longer interesting.

Her family and The Belles were behind her, one hundred percent. She shouldn't marry a man she couldn't love or trust…

Well, one out of two wasn't bad. Right? *Right!*

And it was wonderful the way her friends had rallied. She hadn't spent a night alone since then. She'd had dinner with a different Belle and her loving partner every night.

She was *not* going to cry this time. She wasn't! Just because she felt as if she couldn't go on didn't mean she couldn't survive. She was proving it daily.

"Hey, darlin', can you come back in here now? We've made our decision."

It had only been ten minutes. Julie turned to see Belle's beaming face and the way she was waving Julie's bank proposal about, and she knew it was a done deal.

"It's a deal." Matt put out his hand and shook first Elise's hand, then Brad's.

Elise smiled at him. "How are you feeling? Faint?"

He grinned at his old friend. "Actually, I feel free."

His father and grandfather would be spinning in their graves. But he didn't care. McLachlan, Pettifer and Gardiner Marine Industries was a reality, signed in indelible ink—and he felt like a lifer given parole.

The expectations of a lifetime were done away with. He didn't have to live up to the reputations of his father and grandfather anymore, doing it all and revelling in the control and success at the expense of family life and personal happiness. He didn't have to work insane hours to prove he was good enough. He was free to do what he did best—create new engines and applications—while Elise and Brad backed him up and helped, they were taking the reins of the day-to-day business. They were running the show.

And while the way Julie had left him hurt, while her lack of faith still stung and burned deep inside, he knew that in less than three days, Julie had given him the gift of his life. She'd set him free, in every way. She'd released the man trapped inside the expectations of the heir and the socialite businessman.

He wasn't "A McLachlan", or The McLachlan, anymore. He was just Matt, engineer, father and the man who loved Julie Montgomery with all his heart, and always would.

"Want to go out to celebrate, partner?" Elise asked gently.

With an effort, Matt smiled. "Thanks, Elise, but no. Playing third wheel was never my thing." He lifted a brow, and she blushed and smiled at Brad. They'd only been dating for a few weeks, only starting when Matt's absence had thrown them together, so there was nothing deep or remotely official, but still he was glad for her, glad for them both. "Besides, I have to catch the afternoon train to New York." He patted his pocket to make certain the CD was still there. "I need to run." He shook their hands again. "I'm really glad you're both onboard with this."

"I think this will work brilliantly for all of us." Brad grinned, and Matt knew how close he had come to losing his excellent senior vice president with his too-tight control of the reins of the company.

He'd have to thank Julie for that, too. By showing him where his priorities really were— where he wanted them to be—more lives than his were being made happier.

If only she would talk to him, really talk. If only she believed what he had to tell her.

The worst part was that he could no longer blame her if she didn't believe him. Her parting words had been a revelation. Julie hadn't done a single thing to destroy their love. He'd done it all, brick by working brick, strand by smothering strand.

He didn't even know if he could make it up to her, whether she'd even want it. If she wanted *him* anymore. And he couldn't blame her for that, either.

Julie had been trying to call or see Matt for two days now. She owed him her thanks for the idea that led to her life change, and though she got all the old reactions inside just at the thought of seeing him again, she wouldn't be a coward now. But he wasn't at home, and she hesitated to call his cell number in case he was in meetings or working late. After what she'd said to him, she felt like a hypocrite to interrupt his work to say, Thanks for everything, and all the best with the rest of your life.

But after the call this afternoon from New York, she had to try again. So here she was at eight o'clock on a Friday night, walking up the wide granite stairs to the carved double oak doors. Putting a hand to the real brass bell, over a hundred years old.

Old money, old business, old blue blood. All the reasons why she should never have kissed Matt all those months ago stared her in the face, daring her even to pull that bell.

So of course she did.

He opened the door after the first ring, as if he'd been waiting for her as he had in the old days, and her throat thickened.

But then he just looked at her, as if she were a ghost or a dream. Or a nightmare.

She forced a smile. "Hi, Matt."

"Hi." His gaze was intense on hers. Drinking her in, or committing her to memory? She didn't know. She didn't know what she was doing, either, but it felt too much. Too confusing and beautiful and painful.

"May I come in?"

He opened the door wider, not saying that she could have used her key. She felt relief that she didn't have to make the expected reply or offer to give the key back. Even though it was over, she wasn't ready to sever the final connection with him.

As if he'd heard her thoughts, he smiled, but it was with a clear effort. "Come in. I have things I'd like to show you."

He led her down the hall—a passage seeming empty for once, without prying eyes—and into the living room. And she gasped in delight.

That was why the hall seemed empty! Everything was gone. The portraits of long-dead McLachlans. The antique furniture, the religious carvings from the seventeenth century that were worth a fortune, but whose martyred faces always made her feel depressed. The chintz settings that looked impressive but she couldn't put her feet up on. The Persian rug she'd always been afraid to tred on.

The room no longer looked like a very expensive funeral home. Instead it was full of light and life. A pair of bright, fat sofas with enormous cushions took pride of place around a tiled coffee table sitting on a plush rug that screamed, Roll on me.

And the big screen TV was no longer hung on the wall, but on a massive cupboard with stained rainbow glass doors. Nothing pretentious or screaming understated elegance and wealth. This room yelled, Hi, come and play!

"Oh, Matt," she breathed, taking it all in. "This is amazing."

"You started a revolution inside me," he said, and she could still feel his gaze on her, hooded and hungry. "Once I started changing, I found I couldn't stop."

"You mean there's more?" She couldn't stop staring at the changes…it felt like—like proof, tangible proof…

If only she could believe!

"Come and see." Without touching her, he led the way, taking her into room after room, all light and bright and homey. Even his grandfather's portrait was gone, and the exquisite ten-foot dining table and carved chairs. In their place was—good grief—a ping-pong table! "That was Molly's idea. I eat in the kitchen now," was all he said, leading her into the kitchen to show her the small, round country table and chairs near the back door. "I like it."

"So do I," she breathed, as if it would all vanish if she spoke too loudly.

He didn't smile. He looked as if he was hiding some intense emotion, and she didn't know if she wanted to run a mile, or straight into his arms and hold him until the pain…

How could you end the pain? You started it.

"The hall's still got me stumped, I admit," he said, breaking into her anguish. "I took all the stuff down I didn't like—the cellar's crammed to the ceiling—but I'm not sure yet what to put in. Molly helped me with the rest." He led the way up the stairs…and Julie ached for the times when he'd have been holding her hand, kissing her every few steps, leading her to the bedroom they'd shared.

She'd been living in a fool's paradise then, imagining Matt to be what she'd dreamed in a man.

But now…what was he? He seemed so…so different. And the hooded hunger in his gaze every few seconds as he looked at her…. She could keep her mouth silent, but her body was screaming for his touch, his love. But it was over—wasn't it? She was only here to say goodbye.

When he'd shown her all the changes—beds without canopies and heavy surrounds, simple coverlets thrown over with matching pillows—and they were back in the gorgeously comfy living room, truly now a *living* room… she didn't know what to say except, "It's beautiful, Matt."

"It's a home now, but there's no such thing as a home for one. It's empty with only me here," he said quietly. "Empty without you and Molly here with me to give it life and laughter and love."

Now she really was speechless.

After a while he said, "I guess Ned Pickering called or e-mailed you? Is that why you're here?"

Her throat and heart full to bursting, she could only nod.

"If you don't want to do it, I understand."

"No," she croaked. "I came to thank you. It's…" Tears pooled in her eyes. "You've made a lifetime dream come true. My pictures are going to be published in a book. My own book," she finished in a cracked whisper. "It's…overwhelming."

"Don't thank me. I knew if he didn't take them, another publisher would. All I did was show Ned the pictures you took." He strode over to the French doors, looking out at Molly's kiddie gym and the porch swing. "He grabbed them from my hands and asked who the photographer was. He wanted to make the offer within half an hour."

"Matt…" She shook her head, staring at him, loving his face, hating the pain he wasn't even bothering to hide. "I don't know what to say. There are no words to thank you for all you've done for me."

He gave a short, humourless laugh, still looking outside. "There's nothing to say, Jules. I wanted to do it, to thank you for everything you've given me. For changing my life for the better. For giving me my daughter's love. For loving me once." He turned to her before she could say anything, before she could dash the tears away. He smiled sadly. "That's my Jules. A stray puppy or a kind word can make you cry."

She struggled to smile, and wiped her eyes.

As if unable to stand it, he wheeled away. "I was coming to see you today, anyway. I knew Ned would call, but I have my own news. I sold two-thirds of McLachlan's. It's officially McLachlan, Pettifer and Gardiner Marine Industries." He threw a glance at her over his shoulder. "I wanted to be the one to tell you this time."

Slowly her hand covered her mouth. She stared at him. "But…why?"

"Don't worry, I'm finished with strategies to win you back. I'm done with trying to make you feel what you don't anymore." He put up a hand when she would have spoken. "This time the changes are for me. You made me think when you left. I realised I didn't *want* to go to that meeting. I don't like dealing with corporations. I'm not like my father, a born businessman. I'm happiest creating and leaving the rest of it to others. So, from now on I'll be mostly working from home, or nine-to-five with Elise and my assistants when I need to get into the practicalities. Brad will be handling the business side, with Elise's help. She loves the push and thrust of the business world—and she likes working with Brad and me both. It seemed an ideal solution."

"I'm glad for you." She faltered, feeling as if he'd cut a vein and left her to bleed on the floor. If only he'd done this weeks ago.

He echoed her thoughts. "My only regret is not doing this long ago. Then I'd still have my life with you." He crossed the room to her, standing close enough to touch, but he didn't reach out. "I think you should go," he said roughly, "before I say things you don't want to hear."

Oh, those useless, foolish tears! She nodded, and they spilled over. "Goodbye, Matt," she whispered, gulping and gulping until her throat ached. "I...I hope—"

"Don't say it, Jules. I can't stand to hear it. I'd rather you yelled at me than wish me a happy life without you." He gave a hard, bitter laugh. "I held on to you for as long as I could, but nothing worked. I know you still care, Jules—it's in your eyes, the way you look at me—but it's just not going to work. I made the changes too late."

"It wasn't just you." She gulped again, unable to bear looking at him. "I took for granted that love was enough. But we come from different worlds."

"Yes. You were blessed with a happy childhood with a family that loved you—and I was 'The McLachlan', 'The Heir.' I went to all the right schools, but I never learned to live. Not until you fell at my feet."

Arrested, she looked over her shoulder and slowly turned around.

"Until you, I never realised my parents never even knew me," he said, very quietly, "and I didn't know myself. I kept working, kept piling up money because it was all I knew how to do. That, and listen to them when Father wanted to teach me the business, or Mother wanted to cry. But in all my life, you were the only one who wanted to listen to me because you *cared* about me. I didn't know what to do with it, Julie. I didn't know how to share what was inside me, because I didn't know what was there. Not until you showed me I could be a good father. Not until you took me into your world and I finally felt I belonged somewhere." He looked at his feet. "Not until you left me with only me."

Julie felt herself shaking, biting her lip savagely to stop from crying. Oh, Matt—her beautiful, wonderful Matt! How much of himself, his wants and aspirations, had he learned to hide—because his father, though he loved his son and gave regular affection, wasn't interested in his wishes and hopes, except as it affected his being the heir, not the beloved son. And with his mother, he'd been the adult, the one whose shoulder she cried on, because she couldn't show her pain to the outside world.

"I learned to hide the parts of myself I thought wouldn't be acceptable—less than perfect. Less than expected of 'The McLachlan'," he said, as if a dam had broken and the words were spilling from his soul.

As if he had no one else he trusted to hear his story.

"I become a perfectionist like my father. The things I believed were wrong about my life— like Molly not being my legitimate daughter— I hid from the world. I wasn't ashamed of Molly...I was ashamed of myself, because I couldn't claim her as a McLachlan. My father's problems with McLachlan's became *my* mess, my inherited imperfection, so I never told you about it, either. I only told my mother when it seemed I wouldn't be able to support her or pay the rent on her house. I only told Elise because she could help." His eyes grew more sombre as he kept walking in the darkness of his soul. "But to you, the woman I adore and want to be my wife and the mother of my children, I said nothing, because I couldn't stand to be a failure in your eyes."

She gulped and said, "Matt..." But only her mouth moved; the words still wouldn't come out.

"You said you wanted to know me. This is it. This is me. A stupid jerk who can't stop wanting to be good enough for you. A man who makes all the right changes at all the wrong times." He turned his face from her as he muttered, "I just wish I knew what the hell I'm supposed to do with all this love now you're gone, or how I'm supposed to get through life without you."

She gasped at the suddenness of it, the raw unashamed agony pulsing from him like life-blood. The power of words leashed too long inside the quiet man kept her feet glued to the floor, her gaze stuck on him. She didn't speak. She didn't think she could.

He paced the room a few times, like a caged lion, his hands clenched and his face dead white.

"You can make my day just by smiling at me." He hurled it across the room at her like an insult. "I can be going through hell, but if you smile at me, I *float* through the rest of the day. That's what you do to me with just a smile."

Julie opened her mouth and closed it. Little shots of emotion, shock and hope and long-held-in sweetness, like zaps of static electricity, still wouldn't let her speak.

"Do you know what you do to me with a touch?" He didn't wait for her answer, but went on as if talking to himself. "From the moment I helped you to your feet that first minute it sent shivers down my spine. The power of it still knocks me like a curve ball with more love and wanting than I've known in my life. Even today, when I know it's over, I don't dare touch you. Just being near you leaves me shaking."

Her knees were trembling, too. Afraid she was going to fall down, she hung on to the back of a chair for support, but she couldn't sit. This was a one-sided conversation of such painful honesty it demanded she stand and take it like a woman.

For so long, she'd felt the emotions stored inside Matt, the sense that he was hiding so much from her—but she'd never dreamed it was all about her, *for* her. She'd never dared to hope a man as incredible as Matt could love her so much—plain, red-haired, publicity-shy Julie Montgomery.

"I wish you could see yourself as I see you." His voice was rough with hard-edged emotion. "I see you comparing yourself to Veronica or Elise all the time—your standard of what's beautiful and intelligent. Well, Elise and I didn't work out because she did nothing for me. Kirsten's what the world calls stunning, but she left me because she knew I didn't love her. I thought there was something wrong with me that I could sleep with a woman but my heart was never involved. Then you fell at my feet." He shot her a glance, red-rimmed and brimming with anguish. "You looked at me and fell in love, but you never believed you did the same to me. You honestly believed I could do better than you."

He shook his head, as if she was stupid. "But I see your sweet face as you laugh and love and give to everyone all the time, waiting for me for months without complaint, and I can't believe you ever loved me or thought me worth waiting for. I can't believe you stayed to help with Molly when my stupid kidnap plan must have hurt you so badly."

The look on his face turned hooded again, hungry, drinking her in. "I want to kiss every one of your freckles every time you smile at me. Your curls bounce around in the breeze and I want to lose my hands in them. I love your hair, I love your freckles, I love your face. I love *you*. I look at you and wonder what you ever saw in me. You're so beautiful I *hurt* when I see you."

Her mouth fell open. Her lashes were wet with tears she didn't dare shed. She wouldn't speak, even if she could.

"You thought I didn't tell you about Molly because I didn't trust you, and in a way, you were right," he muttered, eyes dry and burning. "Right from that first moment, you looked at me with all that wonder and trust in your eyes, as if I was perfect. I loved it at first. But I thought that when you found out about her, you'd lose that starry-eyed look and I'd be a schmuck in your eyes, a deadbeat who couldn't get the woman carrying his baby to marry him, who couldn't even make his own kid love him or call him Dad. Then I'd be alone again, having to bear the rest of my life without you. The thought of it—just the thought of losing you—and I couldn't *breathe.*"

Julie couldn't breathe, either. Her world had narrowed to a pair of ice-blue eyes and a pain so bone-deep she wanted to weep, to throw her arms around him and never let go.

"You thought I was locking you out because I didn't tell you about the problems at McLachlan's. Want to know the real reason I never told you, Julie?" He whirled on her, staring with hot, furious eyes, demanding an answer. "Do you?"

He was going to tell her no matter what she said, but he deserved an answer. Shaking, she could only manage a nod.

"When things overwhelmed me, I'd call you or come to see you. I wanted to share it with you, to halve the burden. But when you'd answer the phone or see me, you'd light up with love, and suddenly I couldn't remember why the problems were important. If you loved me, I could fix anything, I could make it through, because you'd be there beside me. They call me a *wunderkind,* but if I am, it's because you inspire me to be my best. I hoped I did the same for you." His chest heaved, but the pallid tint to his face made her doubt he was truly breathing. "'All I want is you,' you said to me when McLachlan's was falling apart. Do you remember that? I hung on to those words like damned jewels for months, but in the end you still left me."

He was shaking visibly now. He wheeled away but continued to talk—throwing the words at her. "In the end, it wasn't you that wasn't enough for me—I wasn't good enough for you. I'm *not* all you want, and you've gone, but I can't stop it. I love you like hell, and now it *is* hell. It's been hell for months, but nothing changes. I'm going to love you for the rest of my life, while you'll find some other guy who can give you whatever it is that will make you happy. But he'll never sell the car he loves to buy you the best diamond he could afford at the time, or see the brilliance in your pictures, or damn well *melt* when he sees you loving his kid. No matter what riches or castles he gives you, he'll never love you like I do!"

Somehow she found her voice. "Matt…"

He didn't hear her; the dam hadn't yet emptied. "What is it you want? More of my time? It's yours whenever you want it. The press gone from our lives? It's a done deal—I've all but disappeared off the radar, or will soon enough. They don't care about simple engineers. You don't like this house? You want a beach house? To live in Australia some of the time? It's so damn ironic—now I can give you the world, but you don't want it if I'm part of the deal, right? You don't want *me*."

"Matt," she whispered, her eyes full of tears and her throat aching, so filled with love she thought it might burst from her physically. The changes to his life were less obvious than the love that inspired it, the lack of resentment that he'd given her all she needed. No—he'd *thanked* her for breaking his heart, and that was all the proof she needed that this was forever. That he'd love her for life. "No, Matt…"

"Don't, Julie," he snarled. "Just go, and leave me here in this house you've helped turn into a home I love at last, knowing you'll never be here to make it...make it—" He swore viciously, using a word she'd never have associated with Matt. He found his way to the fat, stripey sofa as if by instinct, groping with his hands. He sat down and doubled over, burying his head in the crook of his arms. "Just go," he said simply, worn out.

"No. I'm not going anywhere—now or ever." Somehow, even with the tremors filling her body, she reached him, gently shoved him back and climbed onto his lap, her arms around his neck in a similar stranglehold to Molly's. "It's not too late, Matt."

He tried to push her off. "Damn it, Julie, just *go,*" he croaked, his voice thick. "I'm trying to let you go, but I can only take so much!"

Finally words came to her—not pretty words, not beautifully put, but the *right* words to end what wasn't a fairy tale, but a real-life love, a love that would last a lifetime. "Too bad, mate, because you're taking it for life. You're taking *me.*" Her voice choking on tears and laughter, she hugged him hard. "You're marrying me, giving me babies and helping me bring them up. You're growing old with me, and staying with me when I'm grey and fat," she whispered in his ear, before she kissed it. "You'll never get rid of me."

He stilled completely for a few moments. Then he looked up, his eyes bloodshot, face white. "Jules, dear God, don't say it if you don't mean it."

Her heart cracked and burst. "You'll never be perfect, but you're the only man with the power to make me this wretched and this happy, the only man who ever could," she managed to say through a throat thick with tears of joy. "I love you, Matt McLachlan. I have since the day we met, and I always will. You're the love of my life."

Slowly his eyes took fire, glowing from within—and she knew he was beginning to believe. She smiled at him through tear-wet eyes and saw the mirror of her emotion in his. "Oh, damn it, Jules, you're turning me into you."

She kissed him again, this time on the mouth, slow and sweet—but he latched on to her like a starving man, devouring her. She threaded her hands through his hair and kissed him back with all the passion she'd never been able to hide from him, and all the love she'd kept slumbering in some remote part of her heart. "If you say the kind of things you just said to me every day,

I'll never need to doubt your love again," she whispered, playing with his hair.

He stared at her. "You doubted…but I told you I loved you every day."

She shook her head, smiling. "You never said it like you just did—as if you'd rather die than live without me. You always said it so sweetly, so politely, like such a gentleman—such a McLachlan," she said in a frustrated tone that made Matt laugh, longer and louder than she'd ever heard from him—pure, sweet release. "When Jemima Whittaker told me about your success, about Elise and that other woman at our engagement party, and that you were working with Elise, I began to wonder if you really loved me or if I was a burden or convenient. And when you only kidnapped me for Molly's sake, I thought I was right—that you'd never loved me." She bit her lip. "I was even jealous of how much you love Molly," she confessed, ashamed of herself.

"You'll never need to be jealous of anything or anyone again." He kissed her deeply, hot with yearning. "Don't ever doubt how much I love you from now on."

Julie laughed. "After your outburst, I wouldn't dare." She caressed his face, feeling the shaking reaction he'd thrown at her, and another thrill ran through her. "I don't want a polite love. I want *you*, even with all that emotion." She kissed him again. "Especially with all that emotion. Don't change for me, Matt. Don't hide from me, or think what you think or feel will scare me off. Give me you… just as you are."

Slowly he grinned. "If my turning on you like that makes you feel loved, Jules, you can have it every day. It gets exhausting, keeping all that love to myself, anyway."

She laughed and buffed him on the chin. "Then don't, you dope. Talk to me."

"But The McLachlan will come out in me," he said quietly. "Sometimes I'll be distracted or polite, or hide things."

Julie felt her heart melting at the raw confession. "And sometimes I'll be an insecure jerk and test you to your limits. We both have our faults, Matt. And there's nothing wrong with being a McLachlan. Your father loved you, and he didn't do anything to me that I hadn't already done. Part of me never believed I was good enough for you—at least until now." She touched his face, drinking in his skin, loving that she had the right to touch him, with the joy of fingertips. "You're a truly good man who'll do anything to help those he loves. I know I'll have to share you sometimes because of it, and that's okay." She kissed him again, long and deep. "So long as you tell me what you're doing, what you're thinking and feeling, even if it's far from perfect, I'll be a happy woman."

"So I can tell you I adore you?" he growled into the hair covering her throat, nuzzling her through it, and another delicious shiver ran through her. "I can say I haven't slept in weeks without you beside me? That I counted your smiles and laughter like miser's gold, and hung on to every kiss like it was my only hope?"

Could her entire body have turned into one big, enormous smile? "Say it, Matt. Say it all, because I adore you, too." She lifted her face, kissing him again.

"I still don't know why. I've been so blind. I can't believe I never saw you were homesick. I didn't notice how alone you felt while your friends were finding their own men, and I was working day and night. I left you alone to think the worst. I deserved everything you put me through, Jules."

"But I should have told you, trusted you." Another set of soft, sweet kisses. "We need to face all our problems together. I'm your wife, Matt—or I will be soon," she added, soft and dreamy. "So give me everything, good or bad, and I'll be beside you for life, taking all that love with joy, and giving it back in spades."

"Obviously we need to practice our communication a bit more." He nuzzled her lips, smiling. "And thank God we have a lifetime to do it. After the wedding," he said with a wink. "Speaking of which, do we reinstate the wedding or jump ship and elope?"

She laughed with him. "You know, our beautiful friends gave us a priceless gift. It's not their fault the media got involved and things kind of snowballed from there. Let's do it, Matt. Let's smile for the cameras and give The Belles all the advertising they deserve. I don't care how or when we get married, just so long as we do. All I want is you," she said softly, repeating the words of months ago, "to be your wife. Your wife," she said again, just to hear it, filled with love and wonder.

"We'll call them tonight, get things back on track. It shouldn't be too hard, especially if I pay through the nose to get it all back." He held her face in his hands, just looking at her. Drinking her face in as if she was as beautiful as she'd always wanted to be; as beautiful as she now knew she was, seen through the mirror of his eyes. "You're mine for life. I'll never let you go now, Jules, you hear me?"

Not polite, not pretty, but raw words from the heart; and the glow started inside her, radiating outward until she shone. "I hear you…darling," she said softly.

"I love the way you say 'dahling'," he smiled, in loving imitation of her accent. "It drives me crazy."

There was only one way to reward that honesty, and the passion generated saw them slowly tumble to the floor, laughing, kissing, touching.

"I have a final secret for you," he whispered much later, his voice lush and dark with sensuality. "About the wedding. You'll find there were a few…changes."

She sighed and pulled her hands from under his shirt. "Go on." She infused each word with drawn-out long-suffering. "What now, the Archbishop of Canterbury's flying over to perform the service? Did you get the Pope?"

He chuckled and kissed her. "No—I turned it into a 'Matt and Julie' wedding, and long before that damned engagement party."

She gasped, "You didn't! But The Belles—"

"I paid for every change, sweetheart, including the cancellation fees. I made sure they didn't suffer—but I couldn't leave it as it was. I knew you weren't happy with it—and every bride should be happy with her special day. But when I blew it by not telling you everything in time, and then the kidnap went wrong, and you ended up leaving—" he shrugged "—I didn't see the need to tell you."

Julie felt the blush stain her cheeks. "I'm sorry, Matt."

He laid a finger over her lips. "Do you want to hear about our wedding or not?"

She grinned and kissed the finger, softly biting it, and he groaned. "The invitation list was cut by almost half. The cathedral was replaced by a simple service in a Japanese garden, with a marquee for the reception. Only one camera crew and one magazine crew, and only at designated times and places. And we'd found a great chef—he's a true-blue Aussie bloke," he added with a grin, knowing he'd totally botched the Australian accent and not caring. "He's added mini-pies and sausage rolls to the hors-d'oeuvres, just for the Aussie contingent. Not to mention the beer—now what was it called, the one your dad likes? Towey's or something?"

She chuckled, almost giddy with happiness. "It's called Toohey's—darling," she said, just to provoke him. He answered with a passion that left her breathless and aching.

"Anyway, I had your parents ship a few

cartons out, so we can all have a taste of your home, along with some unexpected entertainments. It's all still here. I couldn't bring myself to throw it out." He hugged her. "You're going to have a few little pieces of your homeland at our wedding."

"Oh, *Matt.*" Julie stared at him in wonder and love. "I haven't been home in two years. And with Veronica and Scott's wife, Amy, heavily pregnant, they can't come to the wedding."

"Then why don't we go see them?" He smiled down at her. "We can do Barbados any time. Let's go to Sydney, spend the time with your family."

She hugged him close. "It's winter there now. You don't mind? It's cold in June in Sydney. It's not exactly a fantastic honeymoon destination at the moment, and you'd be sharing me with the family."

"If I'm with you, and you're happy, I don't care if we're in Siberia." He kissed her forehead. "We have a month off. How about we do two weeks somewhere warm and private before we head to Sydney, like the Barrier Reef? Then you get to hear more of your home accent—" he grinned "—we get a honeymoon and family time, and it gives your parents a bit more time to enjoy Boston before they go home." He added, "Actually, we should buy a place in Sydney and live there a few months of every year. You need your family, and I can work anywhere now, so let's do it."

She looked up into his eyes—the eyes she'd fallen in love with at a glance, had never stopped loving for a moment. "I love you," she whispered, with all her heart.

"You know I'd do just about anything to hear those words every day, said just like that," he murmured, kissing her. "You've got me right where you want me."

She felt the shining glow in her smile. "What would you say if I said I wanted us to make a baby soon? I want your child growing inside me— another Molly, with all her adorable attitude."

Masculine urgency filled his eyes and hardened his body. "When? Tonight?"

She brushed her mouth over his. "Give me a year?" she whispered. "I know now what else I want to do with my life, thanks to you. I want to send prints of the photos, and my journal, to the publisher. Then I want to get my travel agent's diploma, set up the honeymoon business and get it on its feet. It's so exciting, thinking of being a real part of what The Belles do. And I have to start thinking about creating the commentary for the book. It's just as well you've organized things with the wedding. You might have simplified your life, but I have a lot to do," she added, half impish, half apologetic, "And as to making a baby, well, it's only a couple of weeks now, and I think it will make our wedding night so much more special if we wait…"

He groaned and buried his face in her neck. "Two more weeks of no sleep."

"You'll sleep," she said confidently, kissing the top of his head, "because now you know how much I love you. Because now you have our wedding, and our life together, to look forward to."

Matt smiled at Julie, twined his fingers through hers, and mouthed *I love you*. She mouthed it back, knowing that this time it really was for life.

The Wedding of the Year, the love of a lifetime, and it was all hers. Matt was all hers. What stronger proof could there be that dreams can come true?

EPILOGUE

Six Weeks Later

JULIE'S veil fluttered around the soft French twist of her hair as she sneaked beneath the bridge spanning a small man-made lake in the Japanese gardens The Belles had chosen for the wedding reception. She looked around and whispered, "Matt?"

"Hey, Jules." Her husband of four hours came out of the shadows, looking magnificent in his tux, the glints of silver shining in his hair in the slants of afternoon sunlight, and smiling with happiness. He pulled her close. "This is fun."

"We have to make kissing assignations at our own wedding. It's so romantic and ridiculous," she murmured with a tiny laugh, angling her head for his kiss.

"Whatever gets me a kiss does it for me." He

kissed her then, long and deep, and she quivered in his arms, feeling so much love and longing it would have frightened her had she not known the same love was hers for life. "We'll be alone soon. They can't follow us to our destination. That's the deal."

"Where *are* we going tonight, darling?" she asked softly.

He growled, "Don't call me *dahling* like that, or I'll drag you out of here and into the big king-sized bed at the bed and breakfast I've booked—the entire building's ours for the night. I can't wait much longer."

She laid her head on his shoulder. "I know. Me either. The last few nights…"

He groaned. "Don't talk about it…at least not until we're in bed. Then you can say whatever you like about how much you want me," he added, tipping up her face with a wolfish grin.

"Want?" she whispered. "This isn't *want* anymore, Matt. It's hunger, craving. I've got to have you. Now." Her hands ran over his body through the layers of his tux, and he strained toward her, groaning. "It's been a perfect day, but I can't stand not being alone with you much longer. I love you so much, Matt. I need you now. Touch me…"

The kiss grew in urgency.

The day had been perfect. The Belles had outdone themselves, following Matt's arrangements to the letter. No change was too small or too big to stop them. The intimacy of the wedding; the unobtrusiveness of the camera crew and the magazine crew, who thought the secret changes to the wedding both romantic and fodder for a great story; the subtle beauty of the reception grounds—an outdoor marquee for the children to play in, along with Australian wildflowers and a band playing classic Aussie hits—had made the day something this homesick bride would remember all her life. Molly's unexpected presence as flower girl, wearing purple and strangling her in a hug, had put the final seal of happiness on her day.

Later, she'd remember it that way. Right now, as touching as the day had been, all she wanted was Matt. All she could think about was Matt…

"Julie—Matt! There you are—and right beneath the bridge, with the sun at a perfect angle, the lilies off to the right. Great photo op! Smile!"

As one, they groaned, smiled at each other, and moved to turn to smile for their dear friend. But the flash had already gone off.

"Perfect." Regina beamed, looking at the back of her digital camera. "Oh, that's the shot of the day. One look is worth more than a thousand words, et cetera!" Still beaming, she came up to them and turned the camera around.

Touching foreheads, smiling with intimacy and joy, Julie's hands still beneath his tux jacket, his hands holding her hips—it was a picture filled with love. And for once Julie didn't care that her hair had slipped from its perfect do, with spirals blowing in the breeze with her veil. She didn't mind that it was as red as ever, or that she could see the freckles on her cheeks, almost glowing with the sun's angle on her skin. She didn't even care that this picture would probably grace the cover of *Boston People Today*.

All she could see was the look on Matt's face, caught for all time. The love her own prince had given her, a very ordinary woman, a real-life fairy-tale ending…

The love would be there for a lifetime, enduring through the ups and downs, the four children in their future, the moves between Boston and Sydney and back, over and over, to show their kids—including Molly—both sides of their heritage, and to end Julie's homesickness for a few months. The love would still be there long after her annoying red faded to grey and she was no longer slender, when she had bifocals and he had thinned hair on top, and a bent back and arthritic fingers from tinkering with new engines.

The picture would appear in the magazine more than once, including on their silver and golden anniversaries. The Wedding of the Year—the marriage of a lifetime.

And the group photo taken by the magazine photographer an hour later, of all The Wedding Belles and their men, would become part of Boston's romantic history too. It would grace the cover of *Boston People Today* more than once. Twenty-five years later readers would love learning about the reunion of friends who eventually parted ways, but whose closeness never faded. Inside the magazine, a massive photo of Belle and Charlie at their simple wedding, six months after Matt and Julie's, and then one of an older group that was present now: Callie and Jared—part-time singer and florist, and full-time professional researcher. Regina and Dell, who still lived in Boston and had spent two decades running their successful photography and jewelry business while raising their children. Serena and Kane, living out in Montana, running a bush pilot service with the help of their two children. Natalie and Cooper, prominent researchers and fundraisers for diabetic research in the tri-state area. Audra would still be managing the finances of The Wedding Belles, while also running an accounting firm full-time, and Dominic's would be one of the most successful businesses in Boston. They would also be parents to three children.

And at the back, smiling, Julie and Matt: part-time Australians, part-time Americans, with their mobile careers—photographer, honeymoon planner, writer and inventor. Parents to five children, including Molly, who would eventually take her father's name and become an "honorary Australian"—part of the Montgomery clan as much as her half- brothers and sisters.

On the second page of the magazine spread a group shot would overflow with the children and grandchildren of six very happy women.

The wedding planners who'd all found their own happy endings.

Celebrate 100 years of pure reading pleasure with Mills & Boon®

To mark our centenary, each month we're publishing a special 100th Birthday Edition. These celebratory editions are packed with extra features and include a FREE bonus story.

Plus, you have the chance to enter a fabulous monthly prize draw. See 100th Birthday Edition books for details.

Now that's worth celebrating!

September 2008
Crazy about her Spanish Boss by Rebecca Winters
Includes FREE bonus story
Rafael's Convenient Proposal

November 2008
**The Rancher's Christmas Baby
by Cathy Gillen Thacker**
Includes FREE bonus story *Baby's First Christmas*

December 2008
One Magical Christmas by Carol Marinelli
Includes FREE bonus story *Emergency at Bayside*

Look for Mills & Boon® 100th Birthday Editions at your favourite bookseller or visit
www.millsandboon.co.uk

FREE!

4 Books
and a surprise gift!

We would like to take this opportunity to thank you for reading this Mills & Boon® book by offering you the chance to take FOUR more specially selected titles from the Romance series absolutely FREE! We're also making this offer to introduce you to the benefits of the Mills & Boon® Book Club—

- ★ **FREE home delivery**
- ★ **FREE gifts and competitions**
- ★ **FREE monthly Newsletter**
- ★ **Exclusive Mills & Boon Book Club offers**
- ★ **Books available before they're in the shops**

Accepting these FREE books and gift places you under no obligation to buy, you may cancel at any time, even after receiving your free shipment. Simply complete your details below and return the entire page to the address below. You don't even need a stamp!

YES! Please send me 4 free Romance books and a surprise gift. I understand that unless you hear from me, I will receive 6 superb new titles every month for just £2.99 each, postage and packing free. I am under no obligation to purchase any books and may cancel my subscription at any time. The free books and gift will be mine to keep in any case.

N8ZEF

Ms/Mrs/Miss/Mr ....Initials ....

Surname ....

Address.. **BLOCK CAPITALS PLEASE**

....

....Postcode ....

Send this whole page to:
UK: FREEPOST CN81, Croydon, CR9 3WZ

Offer valid in UK only and is not available to current Mills & Boon® Book Club subscribers to this series. Overseas and Eire please write for details. We reserve the right to refuse an application and applicants must be aged 18 years or over. Only one application per household. Terms and prices subject to change without notice. Offer expires 30th November 2008. As a result of this application, you may receive offers from Harlequin Mills & Boon and other carefully selected companies. If you would prefer not to share in this opportunity please write to The Data Manager, PO Box 676, Richmond, TW9 1WU.

Mills & Boon® is a registered trademark owned by Harlequin Mills & Boon Limited.
The Mills & Boon® Book Club is being used as a trademark.